D1268867

TALES OF THE
MASTER

- The Book of Stone -

DOUGLAS VINCENT
WESSELMANN

CENTERING CORPORATION
AND
GRIEF DIGEST MAGAZINE
GRIEF RESOURCES

©2015 Douglas Vincent Wesselmann

CIP data available from the Library of Congress

1st printing, August 2015

Published by Centering Corporation
7230 Maple St.
Omaha, NE 68134

www.centering.org to order online.

Contact:
Phone: 866-218-0101
Email: centeringcorp@aol.com

Like us on facebook at: https://www.facebook.com/TalesOfTheMaster
Visit our website at: http://douglaswesselmann.com
Order from: www.centering.org

For Debra, and my Fourth Wife,
and the man who tried to kill me.

What He Will Say:

The imagined barriers of wind
and memory
Are made of the strongest
sun-baked brick.
It is the past that stops the future.
The donkey will not step
because he remembers
the briar in the ditch.
One need not whip the beast,
one need only whisper
in his bent ear,
"Wait, dear donkey,
the smooth stone
of our seeking
was already trod.
What is to come
has already gone,
and thorns await us
as the sun sets
over the eastern mountains.
Man lives only for the future
he has written in the past.
That which I most want,
I have already had.
Take care
to remember the future...

And so I will.
And so I will tell this to you.

Prologue

The baby was dying.

Did I say the baby was dying? I meant the baby was crying. I could hear her. I would usually have gone to her right away. But I thought she was just crying. What I'm trying to say is, I didn't know my baby was dying.

My wife was out. I don't remember where. I was sitting at my computer. I'm a writer and so, you can understand, I was looking for a sentence. I just needed one more sentence. The baby was crying. I was so close to the right words. When I found them inside my head, my fingers put them on the screen, into the file. I hit "save." The words were stored on a chip. That sentence is still on the hard drive. It must be there. Not one single phrase or syllable is left inside my head.

The baby stopped crying.

My wife came home. She went upstairs. I know my wife screamed. I don't think she screamed any real words.

Memory is a strange thing. In my nose, I can still smell the mock orange blossoms in the vase by my desk that day. My fingers still shake with the same tiny tremor that began with that scream. That day, I had a sprig of fresh mint in my tea. I can taste that curious coolness, recall the cold, from tongue, to gullet, to gut, just by thinking back. I don't drink tea anymore.

The baby was dying. I didn't know. I swear.

I

A Plan

It was the last day of my life.

That was the plan. I stood behind the trunk of an old pin oak tree and looked back up the street at my house. There was a dirty yellow Ryder truck backed into the driveway. A woman was shuttling back and forth, from the loading ramp to the front door. She was my wife, but at that moment I watched her as a stranger might, from a comfortable distance.

We'd been living in Sycamore for about four years. I think there was a vague hope that fresh soil would revive us. The grave was only fifty miles away in Omaha. At first, my wife visited the cemetery every weekend. Then she went every three months or so. I went once. The air smelled like river mud and lead.

The woman carried a lamp with a Tiffany shade out of my house and disappeared into the cargo box. At that moment, I couldn't seem to drag her name onto my tongue.

"Cole. Cole." A child's voice. A tug on my pants leg.

I looked down at Ali. I knew his name.

"Cole, take me. Cole, take me." Ali was eight years old. Big Kurdish eyes stared up at me like one of those moist-eyed orphan paintings. The kid and I were both refugees. If I could have liked anyone, I would have liked him. When I first ran into the kid, months ago, I made the mistake of giving him half my chocolate doughnut. Strays never forget food.

"Cole?" He was waiting for a response. Until his family moved here, the only Kurds I had ever seen were distant little specks on a muddy mountain, courtesy of some vaguely guilt-ridden CNN story. Now the mountain had come to Mohammed. They lived next door.

"Okay, Ali. You come with me."

He smiled. All brown skin and white hen's egg teeth.

He pointed at my house. "She's leaving?"

"Yes, she's leaving, Ali."

I grabbed his little hand and tugged him on behind me. Suddenly, I wanted to be on the move. I felt exposed. I didn't want her to see me. The morning was brightening. I needed to put more space between us.

Sycamore, Iowa, has a population of 897 people. The main street, called Antique Row, was still paved in brick. The old pavers only heave up in a couple spots, especially where the big trucks turn off Highway 38 for the grain elevator. Lined by brittle old pin oaks the street was like a tunnel under the branches. Victorian homes flanked the road as it arrowed off the interstate and headed south into uptown. Here in Iowa, we call "downtown," "uptown." Don't ask why. The buildings are old red brick, false fronts, two stories high, neatly painted, and fronted by turn-of-the-century glass globe streetlights. A post office with a winter whipped threadbare flag was flanked by a restaurant and the Legion Hall. The rest of the block was antique stores and two taverns. A block before you get there is Honey's Cafe.

Honey calls everybody "Honey." The farmers gather at the cafe's tables early and catch up on gossip and hash browns. As Ali and I passed by the big front window, all the DeKalb capped heads popped up and took our measure. There wasn't any hostility to it, just a bit of primitive watchfulness. The sense of the moment was like a big dog at his food bowl, stopping mid chew to see who had disturbed his meal. A quick sniff and he starts chewing again.

I didn't know where Ali and I were heading, but uptown was the right direction. A few pickup trucks and cars were moving. The women used their whole hand to make a quick greeting, and they smiled. Men just made quick eye contact from behind the bug splattered windshields, then lifted their pointer fingers. That little one finger move meant acceptance. At least, I took it as such.

We passed the Owl House and it stared at us. The twin-peaked roof with a steep valley, like a beak, running straight to the front, two huge second floor windows like eyes, and Victorian gingerbread that gave the impression of feathers, gave it the look of its namesake. I picked up the pace. A woman lived in the Owl House. I didn't want to run into her today. She had a way of sensing the future.

"Cole! Cole Seatstone, you stop right there!"

"Shit," under my breath.

"Shit," repeated Ali. Not under my breath enough.

Georgia ran toward us. Georgia Jasper, the town intuitive. The windows of the Owl House were eyes, after all. She'd seen us, and now she would torment me.

"Cole, are you all right?" For a second it looked like she intended to run into my arms like lovers in a shampoo commercial. Being the sensitive woman she was, she stopped just short, with her hand on my forearm. "Cole, she's leaving. I saw the truck."

"Yes, Georgia." I didn't like her eyes being this close, or her blond hair smelling so good.

"I predicted she would leave."

"Yes, you did, Georgia." Georgia was always predicting one thing or another. I didn't want her predicting my future. I knew where that day was ending.

"Will you come by later? I know it's hard on you. I could make you some supper."

"Supper," said Ali standing between us.

"No, Georgia."

"But, Cole, you shouldn't be alone."

She didn't know I'd been alone for years. "No, Georgia. I won't be by."

"But we were meant to be..."

"Georgia, don't be crazy."

Her face fell into that trance thing she did when a vision hit her. She would kind of sway and then - and I never figured out how she kept a straight face - she transformed herself into some Twenty-First Century oracle. Personally, I thought the spiel worked best on her internet site. Don't get me wrong, I respected anyone who could make money inventing stories. I was a writer, after all.

"If you don't enter my house," her voice was a monotone, "...there will be a death before midnight." Georgia had spoken. I couldn't help but wonder, was it a prophecy or a threat?

"Death be foe my night," intoned Ali.

"Stop it, Georgia. I don't need your fortune telling. Just stop it."

The gentle seer transformed in a heartbeat. Never call an intuitive a fortune teller. The gifted are a sensitive lot. "Damn you, Cole Seatstone. Damn you."

There was a flash in her eyes and a book in one of her hands. She must have been reading it when she spotted us. Now, she suddenly threw the thin volume at my head. Georgia was slim and athletic. She might have been an all-state athlete, but she was never a team player. Whistling like a power saw blade, the little book would have sliced off the top of my skull like Oddjob's Derby decapitating a garden statue in *Goldfinger*, if I hadn't ducked in time. The spinning tome flew past me and into a bush. A few dry branches snapped as it hit and settled hidden in the hedge.

"Death be foe my night," repeated Ali, as he ran to fetch it.

Georgia spun on her heel and almost ran back into the Owl House. The door slammed behind her, and a cat sleeping in the owl's left eye jumped up to its feet, startled. Then it settled again and stared at me as I stood there on the sidewalk, stunned.

"A death before midnight?" I couldn't believe she had said it. Did she know what I intended to do? Was she foretelling my suicide? "Impossible."

"Impossible," Ali parroted me. His English was still rudimentary. I didn't hold it against him. My Kurdish wasn't very good, either. Ali held out the book he had retrieved from the bushes.

The cover was purple linen, worn, and faded with age. A light, thin thing that couldn't have been more than a hundred pages thick. The edgings of the pages were gilded in gold at one time; now only flecks remained on the sheets. I leafed through the book as Ali and I resumed our walk into uptown.

The printing was dark and large in an archaic font. Rich in curves, and elaborate, I couldn't seem to focus on any individual words until I got to the front of the book. There on the title page, *Tales of the Master: The Book of Stone.*

Ali tugged at my trouser leg. "Read to me. Read to me."

"I don't know, Ali." I glanced up the street. My house was out of sight.

The boy pulled at my free hand and led me to a bench in a small shaded garden on the back side of Stockman's Bank. I don't know why Ali was able to do that to me, to talk me into things. Maybe I was just worn out.

This was where things started to change, though I didn't see it at that moment. Obviously, I wouldn't be telling this odd little story if the plan in my head had been left unaltered. My daughter was gone. My marriage was over. There were no sentences left to write. Everything had fallen apart. Failure is the ultimate soft pillow. My eyes were closed. I was just waiting. Then, well, events, coincidences, and curious bits of the inexplicable started to spin around me. I'll tell the story. Whether it can be believed or not doesn't concern me. I know what happened.

"Read to me," he said again.

We sat down. "Okay. I'll read." I turned past the title page.

Sometimes the most innocent decisions have the most serious consequences. One day, I decided to stay at the museum coffee shop for one more espresso, and I met my wife. One day, I decided to write one more page, and I lost my daughter. One day I held a small purple book in my hand and decided to turn a page.

One day I began to read.

II

The Doctor's Tale

Is this the beginning or the end?

For me, it is an ending. And for you, who have now opened this book, it is perhaps a beginning. This book may lead you.

My name is Finch. Doctor Finch, man of many dreams, of many plans, of many sins. I was rich and I was poor. I knew many things, and I knew nothing. For true wisdom is only wisdom when it echoes into another's ears and then springs new from their mouths. Please pardon my flowery language. The archaic form of this old book has influenced my pen, perhaps excessively.

In a sense, Tadesse found me standing by an open grave. After years of grieving over a mistake, a mistake that left a loved one dead, the thought of death was a welcome comfort.

There were actually black birds spinning long circles in the sky the day we met. Yet, my new friend was smiling. His teeth were white and rounded as a hen's eggs. And he laughed.

"Why are you laughing?" I asked him.

"Because the birds are happy," he said.

"But they are carrion birds."

"And they are happy being what they are."

"They make you happy?"

"Yes, and that I have found you," he said.

Then, Tadesse gave me this small book and he bade me read. This ancient book from Parthia, the wandering tales, supplied many lessons. This simple book was our guide. The grave faded in my mind.

Our wanderings were long. The distances far. Together, we crossed the Atlas Mountains of Africa. We gave food to the Mauretanians. We read books of ancient wonder in Timbuktu. We made salt in the Natal and felt the hatred then burning on the Cape. We found fire in the land of fire and climbed the Andes to the hidden places of the Incas. We made pyramids together with the round-faced people of the Yucatan. We walked through the taiga of Siberia, learning lessons from swarming insects. We passed death camps on Silesian plains and found ruins in Rome.

And I read from this book, as it told my story even before I lived it. I came to understand that there are a million masters. And life was good beyond my imagining. Because I found my Masters and I served them.

And then the time came. We journeyed to the mountains near Kirkuk. There a man betrayed his brother, and a mob gathered to kill him and his. There, as the village burned with a thousand old hatreds, I found the small brown one, my final Master. Know that we brought him here to this land of rolling hills. And with him we brought his mother and his father, the traitor. For it seemed to me that the child should live. Then I returned to the side of my grave because it was my time.

My old friend and Master, Tadesse, said, "Now it is right. For you do not call to the grave, the grave calls to you. And cut out the 'master' crap." He laughed, then, as he always laughed.

Now you have opened this book, this "Book of Stone." Now you will read the tales. My tale is finished. Now you will read the ancient tales. The tales from wanderings before history. Now you will read your story before you can live it. This is my echoed wisdom. My Master told me to remember this well.

And so I have and so I have told this to you.

III

A Request

"Hooey!" I said out loud.

"Hooey!" repeated Ali, with that cosmic smile of his.

"This Doctor Finch was quite a number, huh, Ali?"

"Hooey!" he agreed. I think the boy liked the sound of the word.

I didn't know what it was supposed to be exactly, but I knew enough to spot a crude hoax when I saw it. *Tales of the Master* was a load of hooey.

"Hooey!" Ali did like the word.

Who the hell was this Finch? What was the good Doctor hoping to accomplish with this pseudo-religious treatise? It had to be part of some scam to make money somehow. Was the book intended to be the holy book of some cult? Well, it was a great American tradition to manufacture fantasy. Walt Disney got rich doing it. Doctor Finch was just trying to get his place at the national table with all the other powers that be. Who could blame him for trying?

It was laughable what some people would take to be sacred. I congratulated myself for slipping that trap. I was never fooled by holy men, pure women, or faithful dogs. I didn't trust any of them. I was too smart for that game. I was above all that.

Then, I remembered the bottle of pills I had hidden at home. Finch was thinking about suicide? A coincidence, surely. And the child? I glanced at Ali, then I threw my head back and laughed. For a second I had almost... Then, I saw the black turkey buzzards overhead, circling in the sky. My breath caught. I remember that. But rational thinking took hold again quickly. I laughed again, though it was a bit forced.

I turned the page of the little book.

A poem. Ali spotted it right away. I don't think he could read, but he did recognize the pattern of the words. In a tall narrow column, like a standing stone. Ali had accompanied me into antique store basements before. I'd read him poetry on a couple of occasions. Auden, or Longfellow, or even cummings, he liked poetry.

Ali put his finger on the page next to the words.

"Read! Read!"

"It's hooey, Ali." That was a nice rhyme. "It's hooey, Ali"

He tapped his finger on the page. "Read! Read! Read to Ali! Read!"

There was no escape. "Okay, Ali. I've got some time to kill." I laughed at the ironic nature of my chosen phrase. I read the poem to the little boy tucked under my arm.

My voice seemed to change as I read the words.

IV
Stone of the Master

The Master is within the stone
His body his heart and his soul
The Master is within the stone
His eyes like diamonds and coal
The Master is within the stone
Blood beating as slow as the earth
The Master is within the stone
His being, as sure as a birth

The Master is within the stone
Waiting and watching the road
The Master is within the stone
So pilgrim, here rest your life's load
The Master is within the stone.

For where can your feet go
Walking fast or walking slow
Where can your bare feet go
Where the stone is not below?

V

An Impression

It was doggerel. Not real poetry. I was too smart for this chant.

On the paper, to the eyes, there was a naive charm. Granted, when I read it out loud, the words did hold a little power. The rhythm was like primitive drums. There was a meter there, a simplistic bit of nebulous validity. I didn't trust simple things. I liked Gordian knots and twisted plots and the comfort of doubt.

Ali loved the little poem. But then he loved anything that rhymed. Almost as soon as I finished reading the stanza that ended, "Where can your bare feet go...where the stone is not below?" He stood up and wrapped his arms around my neck.

Hugging me so hard my Adam's apple hurt, he cried out, "The stone. The stone."

Then he let go and recited his favorite poem. I taught it to him the day we found another book by another bard. Ali's face was grave, and his voice dropped to give the verse its power.

He recited it like a prayer. "Candy is dandy. But liquor is quicker."

"Yes, Ali." I agreed. "Liquor is quicker.

"Read more. Do not stop, sir." My God, it was the longest sentence I had ever heard from the boy. "Read more," he said, or maybe he demanded, "Read more."

It was around ten o'clock. The morning was gathering speed. I had so many important things to do. I had to feel sorry for myself. Full blown artistic self-pity could take an hour or two to achieve. I had to go watch my wife pack up the rental truck. That would take an hour of standing across the street with my famous look of desolation on my face, and then an hour of quiet weeping in the garage so that she could hear my despair as she packed up the toaster oven. That could take another couple hours. And of course, I had the suicide note to write. Good prose takes time. I didn't want to dash off a sloppy farewell. I wanted something memorable. An epistle of injustice and loss. I couldn't scrimp on my own eulogy. The first draft alone would take me three hours. Jesus, if I was going to be dead by morning, how could I waste my limited time reading a con man's imitation Torah?

Ali settled in under my arm. His delicate fingers opened the book in my lap and found the page where we had left off. He tapped his finger on the page. "Read Ali more."

I had all sorts of reasons not to, but I started to read again. The distinctions between small purple book and sad little life began to blur.

VI
How It Came to Begin

I am the tall brown one.

My hair is black and its tendrils curl in the wind of Mada. The wind of the dark hills, the wind of the light water and the wind of the desert beyond the great valley flow in my hair. My blood is of the Medes and of the great rivers that shelter man's cities. Yet I live beyond them in a humble dwelling among humble dwellings. I live among those who harvest sweet fragrances in the hills and press sweeter wine in their cool caves.

There I picked blossoms and grapes with my mother and poured wine into jars with my father. There I was a child and there I lived as a child. I was glanced at by young women and their mothers. I was spoken of by the teachers. The people made a plan for me and I bowed to them and the ways of my land.

But there came a day when the small man wandered among us and walked our hills and came to eat at the well. My mother gave him a fresh loaf warm from her hive oven. My sister gave him a fruit from the tall grove below the holy spring. My father gave him a cup of cool beer from the grain in the high meadow. I gave him my ears and the small man filled them through one night and a day.

At the beginning of the second night, my mother came to the well and said to the small man...

"Will you distract my son another night? He must be about his work. The blossoms must be picked. The sweet oils must be prepared and we have need of his hands."

The small man did not answer, but he took what was left of the loaf she had given him, and he crushed it with his heel into the dust.

And my sister came and said to him...

"Will you not free my brother to come and help his people do the labors of the season? I am his sister, and I cannot carry my burden and his."

The small man did not answer, but he bit into the fruit she had given him and pulled out the pit with his teeth. He spit the meat of the fruit into the dust and took the pit in his hand, placing it in a pouch that hung from his belt.

Then my father came and said to him...

"The darkness comes deeper, and my son must rest, for tomorrow there is grain to harvest and grapes to press."

The small man drank of the beer and smashed the cup my father had given him on the stones that line the well. He stood and took my hand in his hand. Then he spoke to me and no other.

"Lead me."

I did not understand. So he spoke again.

"Lead me."

I saw the crust of bread, the muddy fruit, and the broken cup. I felt his hand, and I heard my father's weeping.

"Lead me," the small man said.

And so, on that day's end, in the season of the harvest, I led the small man up the paths past the high meadows. I led him through the half cut fields and beyond to rocky mountains. I have led him ever since that night, for it was meant to be. From his first words, I knew him to be my Master. Now I take my stylus and mark the soft clay. Now I tell of those years. Now I share the tales that I have heard from his lips and passed through with my feet.

These are the Tales of the Master.

VII
Starting

My throat was a little sore from reading out loud.

My voice was suffering from lack of use. I didn't have much to say anymore. There had been a time when I talked all the time. My former friends considered me witty and well-informed; at least I thought they did. I compulsively demonstrated my vocal and mental powers whenever the smallest opportunity arose. But for the last four years, I'd found myself running out of words, running out of quips, running out of friends.

Now here I was, flapping my whiskered jaw to an audience of one; a small boy who probably only understood every tenth word. I wasn't even expending my breath on my own work, I was parroting some deluded text of a long dead con man. I had crossed some line in my life. I wasn't sure what the line was, but I felt my mental tires bump as I ran over it.

Ali was still cuddled in next to me on the park bench. He was warm, and he was looking straight into my eyes. Whether he understood the words I had pronounced or not, he appeared to be transfixed by my voice, by my wisdom, or should I say, the wisdom of the book. Though I am far short of wise and the purple-bound fairy tale was only that – a fairy tale – a fable about two people finding each other. Ali and me? Who was the Master? I almost laughed. That very second was the first second I realized how much I liked this small puzzle in my lap. That bothered me.

Ali was just a young boy. He had that pleasant/unpleasant little boy smell. He was eight years old, but his eyes and his attention span seemed older. It was disconcerting when I thought about it, but I was way too used to being disconcerted by that point to pay it much attention.

I was almost feeling close to the kid. I'd felt that closeness to a child before.

"Get up, Ali. Get off my leg. Get up." I needed him off of my lap. It was a sudden claustrophobic wave. "Get up, Ali!" I almost panicked.

Ali scrambled off me. He had to move quickly, because I was suddenly standing up. I took a couple steps away from him. I felt a little dizzy. Obviously, I'd straightened up too fast. I dropped the book and bent over at the waist. I spent a minute getting my wind back.

When I looked up after my vision cleared, Ali was standing there unperturbed. He showed no concern at all. Like most kids, he obviously hadn't sensed my discomfort. The boy's eyes still held me with a childlike total acceptance. I felt uneasy again.

Ali picked up the book from where I had dropped it. He slowly and precisely straightened out a bent page and then closed the purple cover.

He looked at me again, and holding the book in one hand, he extended his other hand towards me. His voice was clear, less childlike when he spoke. "Lead me."

I laughed. "You were listening, weren't you?"

"Lead me," Ali repeated.

It always amazed me how kids repeat stuff. I had always wanted kids of my own. Be careful what you wish for they said. Long ago, before I got my wish, I doted on a few children. Other people's children. They're always safer. I should have remembered that.

Like my sister's first kid; he was cool. My nephew was two when I got him to repeat "Agamemnon" over and over one day. I was reading him "The Iliad" because I was tired after the third trip through "The Cat in the Hat."

"Agamemnon," I read.

"Aga-mem-non," my nephew returned precisely, syllable by syllable.

"Agamemnon."

"Aga-mem-non." When my sister came home an hour later

we were still going back and forth. That was the last time they let me babysit the tyke. Homer had nothing to do with their decision.

Maybe the same trick would work on Ali. That would be amusing.

"Agamemnon," I said.

"Lead me," said Ali. He held his hand out to me. "Lead me."

Ali was persistent, relentless. I had no energy to deny him.

"Lead me," Ali looked at me like I was the child. I got a little flash again, that the tales were running parallel to my own life. Doctor Finch on the brink of suicide. The brown one and the stranger.

"Lead me," said Ali.

Another flash, I took his hand, and we headed uptown again We passed Iris' Possum Trap Antiques. The odd name was typical for Sycamore. One shop that sold nothing but Christmas related knick-knacks was named "The Easter Store." Go figure. Iris was out front busy with a city boy who seemed to be considering the purchase of a particularly hideous old watercolor depicting Saint Christopher midstream.

"It's a beauty," said Iris. "Look at the lovely blue eyes that Jesus has got."

"I don't know," said the city boy. "I'll look around up the street. Maybe I'll be back."

"Suit yourself. I'll be here." Iris's smile never faded even as the lost customer walked away. She turned her grin on me. "Cole, see you got your shadow with you again today."

"Sure do. Morning, Iris."

"Your wife called. She's looking for you. You oughta go home and talk to her, Cole." She wasn't being a busy body. In a small town everybody's business is everybody's business. That's just the way it is.

"Yeah. Listen, Iris. You know anything about a guy named Finch?" I asked, showing her the little purple book. The biggest danger of asking Iris a question was that you'd get an answer. Every answer lasted a minimum of thirty minutes. During the winter, responses grew even longer. Here at the cusp of the seasons, Iris' reactions would be wildly unpredictable.

"Is that one of Finch's books?" Iris took the book from my hand before I could stop her.

Funny, I had a flash of anger as if she'd just stolen something from me. It passed quickly, but it was an odd feeling. She leafed through it quickly.

"Yeah, that's one of Finch's. Can't read that language it's in, though."

"What do you mean language?" I was confused. I'd just read it and I was strictly monolingual like any good American.

"Weird, I got two new boxes of books in last week. Got 'em from Doctor Finch's estate. Strange books, right up your alley, Cole."

"What kind of books?"

"Phrenology. You know the bumps on the head science stuff."

"Phrenology," I shook my head. Now mankind has always been gullible. We've believed in Astrology, UFOs, Spontaneous Generation, Phlogiston, The Thighmaster, and any number of Presidents from various parties. Mankind has swallowed Chiropractic, High Colonics, Magnetic Sole Inserts, Crystal Power, Pyramid Power, Radon Mediation, and any number of apocalyptic visions presented by various flimflammers. The good Doctor Finch was indeed a con man. What we had here was a little dusty book that revealed all through the systematic study and interpretation of bumps on human heads, Phrenology.

Got a bump on your forehead? You're a criminal. There's an odd bony protuberance behind your left temple? You're a saint. Phrenology, the gateway to the truth about homo sapiens.

Iris sensed the question squatted down inside my head. Even an implied question gets an answer in Sycamore.

"That Doctor Finch was an odd one, and that's sayin' a lot when you consider how many odd ones we've got around here. He was a chiropractor or osteopath or something like that. Bought that farm out there south of the river just before the war. The Nazi War, not this one we got going on now, you understand."

Ali started to reach for some of the brightly colored old tin toys on the sidewalk table. He was fascinated by a green metal Zeppelin with the letters "G O T T" painted on the side.

Iris was gathering momentum. "He paid cash for the place. Not even a check, but cold hard cash. They talked about that at Stockman's Bank for years. They said he made his money back East or maybe overseas. Some said he swindled some rich people in Philadelphia. Well, if you got to swindle somebody, it ought to be somebody rich. Don't you think?"

I was trying not to think. Iris might sense another question.

"He died about two years ago. He was old then. Some folks said he was a hundred but no one really knew. His servant or friend or whatever he was lived on the farm alone after that. He was a black guy. Not an American black, he was some kind of foreign black. Spoke better English than I do, none of that black type talk. Hardly ever came into town. Anyway, the black guy died last fall. Least that's what they think. The grocery man, you know Tommy Dabble, don't you? Tommy found him finally, just before Christmas. He noticed that the grocery bags were piling up on the porch more than usual. Tommy said he found the old man dead in a chair. Just sitting there holding a big rounded stone in his lap. Tommy said it was weird. It didn't smell too bad like you'd expect it to, either."

I started wondering how long it would take until someone found my body. What would it smell like? What would the talk in town be? Hell, my wife was taking all the chairs. I didn't want to be found on the floor.

Iris went on, "Tommy said there was a bunch of really old things, statues and carvings and hieroglyphics and such. Real old stuff. Anyway, I got the bid to do the estate and Tommy was right. There was lots of old, old things. Not the kind of things I can sell here, though. I called up a man at the museum in Omaha. He came in and took most of it off my hands. He probably thinks he swindled me but knowing Doctor Finch's reputation, I figure it was fake, and I got a feeling I swindled him. Besides, I got that Omaha man to buy two tables and a china hutch. I make good money on the big wood items."

"South of town?" I looked off in that direction. I wondered what I could find out there. I don't know why, but it was becoming important to me. The little purple book was burrowing into me.

Iris had a motherly look on her face now. "Yeah, Cole. South of town. But you come in here and call your wife now."

Ali and I, hand in hand, stepped inside. Ali gently retrieved the little book from Iris and I picked up the phone next to the cash register. I just stood there with the phone to my ear. I didn't know what to do.

"Forget your number, Cole?" Iris was understanding. She knew what was going on. The whole town did.

I had forgotten my phone number. There were so many things that I was trying to erase, that I had done a lot of collateral damage. "Yeah," I said.

"Eight, Five, Nine, Nine." There was only one exchange in Sycamore. All you had to do was remember four numbers. Iris was better than the phone company, she knew everyone's number.

"Thanks." I punched the numbers and listened to the ringing. Maybe my wife would be in the truck. Maybe she wouldn't hear the phone. Maybe...

"Hello?" The voice was familiar.

I couldn't seem to speak.

"Hello?" Such a beautiful voice.

"It's me." I wasn't sure what I meant by that. But I'd forced some words out.

"Cole?" Her voice made my throat tighten up.

"Yes."

"I'm packing up the truck."

"I know. Do you need some help?"

"No. I mean, Cole, I don't want to leave without saying goodbye."

"Goodbye."

"I mean in person. Face to face." Was there a catch in her voice, too?

"Okay."

"When? I'll be ready to leave early this afternoon."

"I'll be by then."

"Cole?...."

I hung up.

Iris was staring at me. Ali was holding my hand and the book. We all just looked at each other. The phone rang. I tugged Ali out the front door, and we started running.

Iris called after us, "Cole, it's your wife again! Cole!"

We didn't stop.

"It's important! Cole! Cole Seatstone! She said it's important!" Iris' voice faded as we turned left. We were headed out of town on foot.

We were fugitives. I made it all the way to the corner before I was out of breath. We sat down on the black metal bench in front of the Iron Monger Shop.

Ali thrust the little book into my hand and said, "Read. Read."

What could it hurt? The sun was warm. I couldn't have asked for a better last day.

I opened the Master's book.

VIII
The Tale of the Lost Sons

My Master and I wandered where we wished to wander, and that first wandering was into the mountains of rain and clouds. Those mountains were above the dust and beyond the valley of men. Out of the village of my father we wandered, and for many days we did not speak, for the words were in our steps and not in our mouths.

That day, when it seemed complete, we ceased our journey. The day was white. Snow covered were the mountains where we stopped our seeking. The Master and I entered a cave. He took black rocks into his empty hands, and murmuring beyond my hearing, he made a fire of the black rocks that burned wondrous and warm, so that we sat bare skinned on the floor of the cave. There we shared water, food, and silence for seven days and seven nights. The sun and then the moon appeared to us through the mouth of the cave for seven suns and seven moons. We knew nothing of the world we had left.

For seven days and seven nights we warmed by the fire, and on the eighth morning a man covered in rags entered and spoke to the Master. His face and hands and hair were unwashed, and he spoke to the Master. His voice was harsh with anger, and he spoke to the Master. He drew no warmth from our fire, and he spoke to the Master.

"You brought me here, and now I am lost here. You have gone and you have returned, but I cannot go because I am lost here. You came to my village and took me from my father. You asked me to lead you here, and here I brought you. But you will not lead me home, and now I am lost. Will you lead me now, Master?"

My Master gazed into the fire, and he did not look at the ragged man.

"No, I will not lead you."

And the man wailed so that the cave echoed. And the man turned and went back into the mountain world outside the cave.

And my Master made more of the black stones burn, and we sat again, until on the ninth morning a man in the rich skins of white foxes entered from that world and spoke to the Master. His hair was as white and glowing as the furs he wore, and he spoke to the Master. His eyes looked on our fire without reflecting it, and he spoke to the Master,

"You brought me here, and now I am lost here. You have gone and you have returned, but I cannot go because I am lost here. You came to my village and took me from my mother. You asked me to lead you here, and I brought you. But you will not give me your knowledge of the path, and I am lost. Will you give me your knowledge now, Master?"

My Master stretched out his hands and rubbed them together in the warmth of our fire.

"No, you cannot have my knowledge."

And the man sighed so deeply our flame flickered. And the man turned. In his white fur, he went out into the world of snow.

And my Master and I sat by the black stone fire. I did not speak, but I listened. I listened to the sound of the flame. I listened to the wind going by the cave. I listened to my Master's breathing. I listened to my own heart beating, and time was very slow as I listened.

Then after some days, I know not how many, for I had been listening and not counting, my Master spoke to me.

"They are the lost sons. The son of his father and the son of his mother, they are the lost sons."

My Master spoke and looked at me, expecting my question. I spoke it.

"Did the lost sons lead you here, Master?"

"Yes."

Then, he added more black stones to the fire and melted snow in a small kettle for tea. The tea was brown with the berries from the rock ledge bushes. We gathered the berries as we wandered higher so many days before. I drank of the tea that my Master offered me, and I saw in his eyes that he had a question. Nodding, I accepted it.

My Master spoke, "Does it concern you that they lead me here as you lead me here, and now they are lost?

"I am sorry they are lost."

"Do you fear that you will be lost as they are?"

"No." I replied in truth.

"Do you know the way?" My Master was weighing me.

"No." I stepped upon the unseen scales.

"Do you think I know the way?" My Master held the balance.

"It does not matter." I stood on my feet.

"Why does it not matter?" The final weight was added.

"You are my Master. I seek no way. I will stay by your side." The measure was known.

"And so you shall." My Master was pleased.

My Master smiled as I have seen him smile so many times, but this was the first. He offered me more tea, and then still more. Together, my Master and I became drunk on the strange flavors, and I saw many things that were not real and many things that were, and together we laughed. We slept by that black stone fire, and when we awoke we went out of that cave.

My Master spoke, "My head hurts from last night's tea and this morning's sun."

Together we laughed, and he held his hand out to mine.

"Lead me. And remember well the lost sons."

And so I did.

And so I have, and so I have told this to you.

IX
Walking on Gravel

It's impossible to lose your way when you don't know where you're going.

I had finished the tale. In the back of my mind, I began to chew on the moral of the story. It wasn't hard to admit that I was a lost soul. But I hated sermons. I wanted an answer, not a lesson. Truth was, I realized, I wanted punishment without a lecture. If the little book kept hitting so close to home, I might have to burn it along with the last bridge behind me. Then out of the corner of my eye, I saw Iris emerge around the corner and look our way.

"Cole, your wife called again!" She'd spotted me.

As usual, I was being driven by circumstance. Ali and I jumped up off the iron bench and took off as if we were pursued. The sad fact was, no one cared enough to chase us. Ali was just along for the ride. His little legs spinning away like a cartoon character, he was keeping up, but barely. I tugged him down the block and around the corner onto the bridge.

Uptown Sycamore ended at the river and the bridge. The majestic trickle of the Elk River was spanned by a monumentally Stalinist slab of concrete known imaginatively as Town Bridge. The narrow gray arch stretched over the gully had replaced an old wooden covered bridge. The town council had ripped down the old landmark just before an Iowa boy penned his elegy to its teetering kind. The decision was a classic bit of poor timing. Now tourists were thick as feedlot flies the next county over. Out of state plates flocked to the rival town of Plank City in the summer to reaffirm the romance of pickup trucks and older outlaws with cameras and the fantasy of a half naked Meryl Streep. Nobody seemed to care that the bridge in

Plank City was only ten years old. Nothing lets us suspend our sense of disbelief quicker than a bestseller.

The two of us slowed about halfway across. Ali giggled as I panted. He mimicked me holding my side in pain. His delight in the whole situation was contagious. I found myself laughing, too.

I walked to the railing and looked down into the paltry little stream below. Ali boosted himself with his skinny arms and took his own gander. Tall dry grass matted down by winter snow choked the waterbed. A muddy meander twisted across the mostly empty stream bed. Ali and I decided simultaneously to do what had to be done. We spit.

Ali turned to me with saliva dripping off his chin. "Spit!"

His vocabulary was bigger than I thought. "Spit," I agreed.

"Spit!" So he spat.

So I spat. "Spit!"

Ali spit over the edge again.

I spit over the edge again.

He spit.

I spat.

There was spit all over the railing, and I started to laugh.

A big grain truck rumbled by. It was dusty on the bridge, and narrow. My accomplice and I headed across. In thirty-six steps, I counted, we were in the country. The ditch weeds had dried out in the winter winds, and ugly grackles were foraging through the rustling stands, looking for an early spring meal. They scattered as we approached and reformed the cluster when we had passed.

I didn't know where I was going, but Ali held my hand, and the slope up from the river was gentle, so we walked. After another grain truck sped by with its wall of wind, I decided to get off the highway. I turned onto a gravel road. Ali followed.

Two or three hundred yards off the main road, I started to notice the rhythm of our feet on the white gravel. A heavy crunch, light crunch, light crunch, heavy crunch, light crunch, light crunch, heavy crunch... like the pattern of drums at a military funeral. After two or three hundred yards more it was a chant. After another three hundred yards it was a song.

I started to hum, and Ali joined me.

Ali knew the words to the song. "...A three hour cruise...a three hour cruise...a three hour cruise...a three hour cruise..." For a second there, he even looked a little like a miniature Gilligan.

I was just starting to wonder if I was the Skipper, when I saw a dog beside the road. It was lost dog ragged. The fur and mud were blended and indistinguishable. The bare spots showed bone under weeping skin. The dog was beyond starvation. I remembered a half eaten piece of jerky in my sweater pocket. I retrieved it and held it out towards the animal. He circled me but could not bring himself to step within three feet, about the range of a man's kick. The dog had learned to measure the reach of pain.

I tossed the lint-covered beef over the invisible wall that kept him from me. The dog sniffed at it and finally took it in his mouth. His jaw spasmed, and the jerky fell out onto the road again. The dog was too weak to eat. He'd endured the winter but had no strength left for spring. Nature would take its course. Like me, the poor thing would welcome the comfort of an ending.

Another hundred yards and there was another dog. It was filthy white with gravel dust. The mutt was huddled in a thicket of dead sumac, and as we approached, it struggled to get up. Something was wrong with the poor thing's rear legs.

People from the city dumped their unwanted pets out here all the time. The dog pooped too much. The dog barked too much. The dog ate too much. Somebody was moving. Somebody was bored. Somebody was cruel. They drove them out into the country and kicked the dogs out the door. The countryside was full of these refugees.

I approached the whimpering thing. I had some vague notion of helping. As I reached my hand out to comfort the dog, it snapped at me. I felt vicious air on my fingertips as the teeth missed me. I backed up. I could give no help. No help could be accepted. This dog had learned its lesson about humans. The mutt knew their smell. I had the scent of pain on me. Dogs are keen in their judgment.

The two strays had learned the wrong lesson, like the Lost Sons. The connection clicked in my head. Like the Lost Sons, we all learn the wrong lessons. Two lost dogs and two lost sons, one could not be fed, and one could not be carried.

"Weird." I said it out loud as the connection was made.

"Weird," echoed Ali.

We walked away. Crunch, crunch, crunch on the gravel, until the song returned.

Ali sang again. "...The millionaire and his wife....the millionaire and his wife...the millionaire and his wife..."

I regained my current level of almost sanity and realized I was imagining any connection between the *Tales of the Master* and the suffering animals. The sensation had to be a residual marijuana flashback reverb time loop defect in my formerly chemically abused head. There was no connection between them or me or my life and this "master" thing. True, I was suicidal, but I hoped I wasn't nuts. Killing yourself should always be a rational decision.

There was no lesson here, except that people were cruel. The dog was right. They'd been cruel to me. Even my friends had been cruel. They offered no help. They weren't there to catch me when I fell. God? Well, God was a concept, as Lennon would have said, that didn't enter into this little internal discussion.

There was no wisdom in the little book, no lesson in this little slice of life. Except perhaps that some people are gullible, and some people are cruel, and dogs and babies die in the spring. The crunching of our feet became anger in my head.

Ali kept singing, "...And his wife...and his wife...and his wife..."

I didn't want to scream at the kid, so I led him off the road through a gate and sat down on the sun struck side of a pin oak. The soil was soft. The field was full of the nose-filling air that is only found around farms.

Ali sat down beside me. His eyes locked on me, waiting.

I opened the book, and my voice sent the next tale out across the waiting meadow.

Ali's ears perked for the new sounds.

X

Tale of the Flower, the Dove, and the Woman

We rested that day, and my Master had removed his robe. He used it as a pillow. He placed his back against a warm black rock on top of a small peak. The day was blue. It was a time my Master blessed me with his ears and listened to my questions.

The sun warmed us. The breeze was on our skin. I spoke in respect.

"What is the difference between wonder and magic?" I said.

He showed his teeth in a smile upon me. They were like chicken eggs, round and white.

My Master gestured with his hand. His fingers curled and uncurled. His hand was empty. He curled and uncurled his fingers again, and in his palm there was a tiny blue flower. He gave it into my hand.

The flower's blue was as lapis lazuli. There was gold in its center, and its stem was the green of a lizard after desert rain.

He reached his hand into the air again, and uncurling his fingers, a dove was revealed, white as a flock of sheep on a meadowed hillside. The bird turned its head and looked into my eyes. I trembled as it jumped onto my finger where it alighted without weight.

My eyes did not blink as the dove took the flower in its yellow beak and stretched its wings. The dove took to the air and flew up into the sun until I could see it no more.

I began to speak, but my Master gestured me to quiet.

He extended his hand again, and my eyes followed as his finger pointed down the hill. I beheld a woman standing in the shallows of a sandy pool. She was bent at the waist, and her hair was in the water as she washed it. The woman straightened, and clear water cascaded from her long black hair. The water flowed across her shoulders and down her body. It splashed back into the pool, and the woman smiled. Brown skin, black hair, and silver water under the sun.

My Master spoke, but my eyes were on the woman in the pool.

His words, "The flower and the dove from my empty hand are wonders. They cannot be explained. They fill your mind with questions. From whence did they come? Where did they fly?"

His words filled my ears. "As you behold the woman your mind is empty. Your soul is filled. There are no questions, only a host of answers. You see all the answers in her. That is her magic; an answer without a question."

"A wonder will amaze you."

Spoke my Master, "Magic will change you."

Spoke he, "Take care to remember."

My Master closed his eyes and dozed under the sun, on his robe and black rock. "Take care to remember this."

And so I have, and so I have told this to you.

XI
A Trick and a Truth

I closed the book slowly, my eyes alert for magic birds and topless women.

There were none in sight. There was only Ali. Our butts were in the dirt. We were leaning on the tree, occasionally scratching our backs on the bark. Big bear and little bear, emerging from the winter.

"*Tales of the Master*," I said dismissively.

Ali aped me again. "*Tales of the Master*."

Just for a moment, I had hesitated on the edge of thinking the book was pushing me. Just for a moment, I caught a glimpse of me in a *Twilight Zone* episode. I started to think there was wisdom for me in this charlatan's charming bit of forged folklore. Just for a moment I thought...

"Magic?" I asked Ali.

He lit up. Did he understand? "Magic," he said.

"Magic." I curled and uncurled my fingers. My hand was empty. I placed my hand in front of Ali's expectant eyes. I uncurled my fingers and curled them and, "Alakazam!" I had his nose.

Ali's eyes were wide. "Wonder." He was amazed. "Wonder."

I displayed his captured nose. "No, Ali. Not wonder... Magic!"

"Wonder," insisted the boy.

I popped his nose into my mouth and swiftly chewed it up. I swallowed his nose.

"Wonder," he said again.

I reached behind his ear, and, "Presto!" I revealed his nose yet again.

"Magic, Ali. Magic."

His face was full of sunlight and he said, "She loves you."

The words leapt out of his mouth and thundered into my head.

"She loves you," said Ali.

What did he say? "Ali, what did you say?"

He looked at me and reached out to my hand. He peeled back my fist and retrieved his nose. The brown boy put his brown nose back on his brown face, oh, so gently. Then he said to me, "Wonder."

I knew I had heard it. "She loves you." I had heard him say it. Was it true? Was it magic?

I opened the book.

XII
The Tale of the Protector

The wind blew that day, and my Master's robe flowed with air and dust.
The day was yellow. I urged my Master for a rest.

"Can we not turn our backs to this cold intruder? Let us turn back, or if
you are willing, stop and await the quiet time."

The wind and dust increased.

He remained silent and only walked on across the dry brown grass.
The length of his stride did not slacken. I had learned to wait. My Master
had taught me this in his silence. After a time, he whistled like a flock of
birds, sky turning as a living drop of feathers in the autumn ocean.
Then he spoke to me.

I saw his face again. My Master was smiling and full of a story.

And thus he spoke:

In a certain village, between a hill and a stream, there was a man who
made boots. For many years, he had fed his children and blessed his wife
with servants from the money he made selling his handcrafted goods.
Fortune had given him four sons. Each was more noble than the valley
had seen in its sons for many harvests. And his two daughters had faces
full of wisdom. The man's daughters were renowned beyond the hill,
beyond the stream.

The sun was warm in those days, and the rain was well given.
Wealth flowed to the man, and around him it flowed to others.
The man's sons walked through the village, and all shared in their beauty
and playfulness. People from all over the village gathered at his table,

and the food tasted of friendship. Songs were sung that gladdened all their hearts. Man and woman could look at each other then.

Yet there was a darkness. In the man's heart stirred a thought like a snake.

And the rich man said to himself, "As I look around me, my eyes see my riches, my sons at their games, my daughters with their people. And all around, I see growing things. I know from my readings of the men in the deserts and the envy that they hold in their hearts. For the men in the deserts have little, and they burn like their sun for cool water. Their ears listen on the wind for word and rumor of the coolness of my well. When they hear of me, they will come. They will come hunting, and my sons will die in innocence, my daughters perish in fire. Surely I must meet them before they reach my beam and door."

And the man of that living village took up his staff and went out.
He sought out the ones who have knowledge of killing men. I shall not utter their names, for they are names of dying music. He sought them out and learned from their voices. The man lingered with them across many seasons. He learned well and deep, until he was beyond his teachers.

Then he traveled again, and he traveled towards that desert land.
And now his staff was no longer wood. His staff was steel that reached tall in his hand. For many long seasons he wandered the land under the sun, and he used his knowledge. He killed them in their houses and alone on their roads. He killed those who coveted what was his. Those who dreamed of his daughters, he killed. Those who would deny his sons, he killed.

The man's eyes were the last of men's eyes to look upon that wavering sky. For when he left that land, that land was empty.

So he set his feet on the road that led to hill and stream. Sore tired, he took his steps, and long was that journey. After many days, his eyes again saw his village. The thought, like a snake, had grown and whispered to him.

The snake said to him, "The men of the marsh have little. They shiver like the ice for warm hands of woman. Their ears listen in the ripples for word and rumor of the warmth and smoothness of your bed and hearth.

When they hear, they will come."

And the man's son's said to him, "Stay, father, for the harvest is in our bins and there is feasting."

And his daughters said to him, "Stay, father, our song for you is finished. Hear us sing."

But the man knew the danger. He had seen it in the men of the desert and in their eyes. Now, he went on and sought the men of the marsh with his steel. They fell before him, and the reeds grew on without thinning from that day.

Next, the men of the mountain and the men of the sea fell before him, for the man had learned to kill, and his steel could not be stopped. The men of the forest and the men of the rocks fell before him, for he saw their dreams. The men of the harbor and the men of the farms, they all fell before him.

When there were none remaining, the man returned to his village between the hill and the stream. There in the middle of his village, he finally stopped his feet. His steel staff was scored and bloody. And his eyes beheld his home once more.

The bushes were dry. The rains had not been given. There were no people at his table for it was bare and there were no crumbs upon it. The beam of his house had cracked with dry, and the doorway eaten by beetles. In fear, he called to his wife, but she no longer knew his voice.

He called to his sons, and they spoke to him.

"We have been warned by our father against the men of this earth. We do not know you."

And he called to his daughters, and they spoke to him.

"We have a song for our father, but you are not he."

And the man's sons he allowed close. Whereupon they fell on him and stabbed him with their rusted knives that had no meat to cut. His sons and daughters left the man to die. They did not know him. His body was not buried. The man's body remained in the middle of the poor village, as if invisible. And the people searched for food, never seeing the blood and the ruin of their own father. And there was no food.

At this my Master whistled again like a thousand birds and strode on. At that time, the wind had stopped blowing. The wind had blown a day and a night and one gust besides.

I asked my Master:

"Master, what does the story mean?"

My Master smiled.

"The man became dust. His sons became dust. His daughters and his village are no more. You complained of the wind. It was merely all of them passing by. Do you think of this as a sad story? There was sadness. But the sadness was in the ending. The sadness passed us in the first gust of wind."

"Did you miss the joy of those years before the steel? They passed by in the wind of a day and a night. The happiness passed us in abundance. Take care to remember."

And so I have, and so I have told this to you.

XIII
A Portrait

The Tale was not what I wanted to hear.

Ali had clearly said, "She loves you." That had been magic. What was this next bloody screed about? An anti-war parable was not what I needed. My wife was leaving me. Did she love me? That's what I wanted to find out. Now, instead of enlightenment, this creepy ersatz testament told me about a man and his ungrateful children. I couldn't figure out what I was missing.

Hell, I didn't care if she loved me. After that one single minute, that moment four years ago, that second when our child's gentle breath had stopped, that instant when silence arrived, I had set out to prove that she did not love me anymore. I had proved it. She was leaving.

I'd had it with books.

We had moved to Sycamore to simplify. After everything happened, my writing stalled. My editor thought my new novel was depressing. My readers agreed. We sold the big house in the city and moved to this farming hamlet to find me peace. I would be able to write again. I'd be able to find the next sentence.

It was an insane idea. Being a writer means you've got to have the tenacity of a bulldog, the patience of a bloodhound, the energy of a Chihuahua, the self-confidence of a Rottweiler, the inner peace of a schnauzer and the vision of a Maltese. I'm nothing like a dog. Rub me on the belly and I plunge into an ill-defined world of repressed trauma and recovered memories of childhood episodes of severe swimmer's ear. If I'm anything like a dog, I'm a Heinz 57 locked in a car on a hundred degree day. I'm good at writing, but I'm terrible at being a writer. It's an important distinction. And then I had ignored a baby crying.

I just kept sinking. I took my marriage with me.

I threw the book into the field. It skipped like a stone off the clumps of newly thawed dirt. Ali ran to fetch it, and I stood and stomped off back to the road. Back to the gravel, the reassuringly real gravel.

Where was the magic of the book? Typical, I had started to believe... I didn't know what I had started to believe. Jesus, I almost got sucked in. Faith was a vice I wanted to avoid. I heard Ali's feet scrambling on the road to catch me. I didn't wait for him. I just walked. I counted a thousand steps before he caught me. I was finished crying by then.

Ali took my hand, and our pace slowed. I needed to get back to town. My wife was there loading a yellow truck. I could be there. I deserved to watch her go. Then I would die. I had to get back to town. Then I saw the mailbox ahead of me on the road. I saw the name on the mailbox.

"Dr. Finch." The name was in black letters. There was a bullet hole dotting the "i." So, this is where the mysterious doctor and his black foreign friend had lived. This is where the book came from. The coincidences were piling up.

There was a short lane leading up a small wooded hill to the farmstead. The yard was overgrown. The old barn, brown and leaning badly, was next to a decapitated brick silo that had a tree bravely venturing out of the broken crown. A wheel-less rusted jeep sat on concrete blocks under a giant budding lilac bush. Rusty vehicles on props are almost an artistic convention on Iowa farmsteads. The big frame house was half-white; most of the paint had long ago flaked and powdered. A picket fence had only half its slats, and the front porch sagged when we stepped up towards the door. The door was open.

Dust swirled around our feet in the front room. A cloud of it climbed into the stale air, pushed by the slight breeze of the heavy carved oak door open behind us. A stairway was straight in front of us, heading up to the second floor. The bannister had been stripped away. Iris made money off the wood items.

To my right was an empty parlor with patches of broken

plaster on the floor. The walls were cracked. There were spaces where pictures had hung, now just negative shadows. Another room beyond was marked by water that had defeated the roof and invaded the house long ago. In spots, salvageable wood had been stripped off the floor. I had to step carefully. Next to the kitchen was a pile of old copper pipes torn out and ready to sell, and to the left, another room with a fireplace. The mantelpiece was marble. Someone had tried to remove it, but the side columns had cracked, and the effort had been abandoned. In front of the hearth was an old bug-eaten overstuffed chair. There was a slight sweet smell mixed with the dust there.

This was where they found Doctor Finch's man. I knew it. He had died in this chair. Sitting on the floor next to the ottoman was a stone. About six inches in diameter and two inches thick, tapering to a rounded edge; this was the stone they had found in his dead lap. A lonely death, shared only with a rock. I picked up the stone, and it was smooth and warm like sand in bright sun. I remember thinking that maybe I'd hold the stone in my own lap that night when the end came.

I felt such sadness there.

Sticking out from under the derelict chair was the corner of a brown folder or something. I pulled it out and brushed the dust and lint and cushion stuffing off the cracked cover. It wasn't a folder, it was an old photo album. Most of the pages had separated from the binding. There were only four water stained and torn sheets left. Lord knew what had happened to the rest. Seven or eight yellowed black and white photographs clung to their mountings. One was a picture of a tall, young, wavy-haired man in classic colonial khaki, standing in front of a shiny new jeep, next to a tumbled pile of broken mud bricks and three battered palms. The photo was captioned, "UR 1963." Another showed the same man and jeep, older now. The jeep was dusty, the man was graying and backed by a lush landscape, a small black boy sat on the jeep's roof, grinning from ear to ear. There was something familiar about the boy's teeth. I couldn't place it, just something familiar.

The other photos, uncaptioned, were of the tall man and the

black man. The kid had grown up. The two obviously liked each other and obviously traveled all over the world. They were in front of the pyramids, the Eiffel Tower, snow-capped mountains, on a ship. They both had dazzling smiles. The last photo was glued to the inside of the back cover. It was the only one that was in color, obviously the newest of the collection, barely worn at all, and not a bit yellowed. The tall gray haired man must have taken the shot because I couldn't see him. The black man, much older now, was standing on a muddy road on a mountainside. The jeep, now rusty, was behind them. Two grown figures were wrapped in blankets in the back. The black man was holding a baby. The odd thing about it was the way both of them, black man and infant, stared straight into the camera. Their eyes were piercing. I got that deja vu again.

Then I heard Ali, and he was laughing. The sound came from upstairs. I had lost track of him. The laughter of a child seemed out of place. The giggles seemed wrong. I ran upstairs and was led to a back bedroom. There was Ali dancing, stirring up great clouds of dust and pointing at a picture on the wall. Hanging at an angle, the portrait was missing half its ornately carved frame. Ali pointed and laughed.

Through his laughter he shouted, "...the fearless crew! ...the fearless crew!"

With all the dust suspended in the air and sparkling in the shaft of sunlight coming through the torn blind in the broken window, I had to get close to see the faces clearly. As the image became clear, I started to smile.

The late morning sun framed the oil portrait. A man and a boy, seated on opposite sides of a small table, looked at each other. The man was white-haired and distinguished in a black coat and cravat. The little boy was as black as the Sudan and clad in a white jacket. The man had his thumbs stuck firmly in his ears. His fingers were extended like flapping wings. His eyes were crossed, and he was sticking out his tongue. The boy, a little black boy, was holding a green toy zeppelin in his baby fat fingers. The letters "G O T T" were painted on the side, and the child held the metal plaything like a cigar. The boy was wearing a big red ball on his nose, and his mouth was open, his eyes wide in sheer hilarity. On the table stood a white frosted cake, and atop it was a rooster. The bird's beak was covered with icing, and his eyes looked straight at me in puzzlement. I had never seen anything like it, the painting of Doctor Finch and his man as a boy.

Ali was pure merriment, dancing and singing, "...The fearless crew!... the fearless crew!"

I laughed and agreed. "Right you are, little buddy. Right you are." I was laughing again on a day I had been sure would be laughter free. Then the dust made me cough. The harder I coughed, the more Ali laughed.

I laughed and coughed, and we retreated downstairs and onto the porch. My lungs finally cleared. Ali hugged me and laughed, and I hugged him and laughed. I had taken the picture down, and now I knocked off the last of the frame and gently rolled up the canvas. I wanted it.

"Whatcha got there, Cole?" It was one of Iris' sons. She had two boys. Frank was fat, but friendly. Iris' other son Bobby was fat and mean.

I was startled by his sudden presence. "Frank?" I hoped it was Frank, not Bobby.

"Whatcha got there, Cole?" It was Frank; Bobby would have hit me by now. He had before.

I looked down at the rolled up painting in my hand. "Just lookin' around, Frank. I found this old picture." I unrolled it a bit to show him.

"That? You can have it. We got everything out worth selling. I just came back for the last of the copper pipes. You walk out here?" Frank was looking at Ali. "You walk out here with him, Cole?"

"Yeah, sure. He's my partner," I said.

"You wanna ride back to town? Looks like your partner could use some lunch." He was right. It was almost noon, and Ali always looked malnourished.

"Sure, we'll take that ride."

"Just wait up, and I'll load the pipe. Sad old ruin, ain't it?"

"Yeah," I agreed. But in my head, I understood the tale now. Doctor Finch's house was much more than a rundown memory. Its past was much more than its now. Was that the lesson? I wondered. Truth is, at that point, I was unsure of almost everything. I was growing very uncomfortable on a day I had been sure would end in the bliss of certainty. Now, as the book paralleled my life, more and more obviously, my illusion of clarity was slipping away.

The noon whistle screamed out from town. Out here, on the abandoned farmstead, it sounded menacing.

I helped Frank toss the salvage into the bed of his old International pickup. Then Ali and I piled in. I checked my pocket to make sure I still had the book and that curious rounded stone. Having the stone seemed to be important. At the time, I didn't know why.

The conditions in the truck's cab were cramped. Frank was broad at the bottom. But it was a short ride into town. We crossed the bridge, and Frank pulled up in front of the Possum Trap.

"Thanks for the ride."

"No problem, Cole." Frank mussed Ali's black hair before we could escape.

After we made it out of range, Ali said, pointing at Frank's retreating form, "Skipper. Fat Skipper."

I laughed.

Ali handed me the book. There were more tales to be read. I needed another before I went back to my house. I needed to know. Or maybe I was stalling. Right around that time was when my motivations all became tangled; babies, trucks, books, and a little brown boy. We settled on a bench. I opened the book of tales.

Ali urged me on. "Read. Read," he said.

The title of the tale startled me.

XIV
The Tale of the Four Wives

Coming down from the mountains we walked in laughter. And the day was half yellow.

And as we walked, I saw with my eyes the beauty of this forest beyond the mountains. For there were trees like pyramids and trees like domes of turquoise. There were grasses and grains and vineyards that filled me to amazement.

My Master, too, saw it as for the first time, though he had walked this road many times. He whistled then a song of yellow-feathered birds. Some flocks of those birds began to shadow our path as we followed the trail through this sunlight and green glowing land.

After a time the road turned, and at a carved trunk of eldar, split two ways. One way led towards a waterfall and a village of wooden houses, fine in their construction, and the other led up into flowered willows and a villa that glowed with a golden roof.

Laughter and singing could be heard coming up from the village. From the villa came the incense of mourning. The sweet smell of burning cloves, used by wise physicians to free the soul from a failing body, was on the breeze. And this was the place of a choosing.

I looked to my Master but he said, "As you will. There is dancing in the town. There is death in the house. As you will."

I listened to the songs below, and my nose was filled with the smoke of dying from above. I searched my heart as I faced the choice.

And my Master spoke, "Do not search. Do not listen. Choose."

My right foot moved up, and my left foot followed, and so I found myself in front of the golden villa. The door was open, and an urn full of water had been spilled on the threshold, for there it is believed that demons may not cross water. The house smelled of burning cloves, and in the great room before me, a man lay on a yellow-sheeted pallet. His face was as ashes and his brow lined in pain. Beneath his head were purple pillows, and the smoking brazier at his feet was surrounded by three physicians dressed in the robes of wise healers.

I spoke to these noble men, "Tell me physicians. Is this man dying?"

And the first of them, with bejeweled fingers, said to me, "My art will bring him life."

And the second of them, with silken belt, said to me, "My skill will bring him potency."

And the third of them, with rouge and rich sea beads, said to me, "My pillows will bring him comfort."

The man with the face of ashes was covered by the shroud's light yellow of sweet mountain flowers, and he gestured to me. Approaching, I bowed, for he was a powerful man and rich past what I had seen in my short time in this world. He took my hand, and I brought my face to his. He spoke faintly to me.

"Stranger, bid the doctors leave. Pour more water on my door, and summon my wives."

I did as he requested, for the wishes of the dying are a command among my people. I set the doctors on the road under the flowering willows and poured water on his door sill. I knocked at the women's door, carved with antelope and lotus. I bid his wives attend him, and his four wives moved, one by one to his side, through the veil of clove.

The first wife approached, and I heard them speak. Man and wife. "Oh, wife of many years, I have honored you every day by all of the rituals. I have respected the forms and the commands you have given me. Will you now go where I must go?"

The first wife said, "Husband, you have observed the customs. You have kept your word to me through all of the years. But I will not go with you, for I cannot. The law that binds us is of paper, it will be consumed in your pyre." The first wife backed away from his bed, slowly and respectfully.

The second wife approached, and I heard them speak. Man and wife.

"Oh wife, I have given you jewels. I have provided you with hearth and home. I have worked and given you servants to honor you. Will you go with me now to where I must go?"

The second wife spoke, "Husband, you have given me much and taken little. I am heavy with your gifts. The weight of these riches binds me so that I can no longer move as I will. I cannot go with you because you have made of me this world."

The second wife turned and ran into the arms of a younger lover. They embraced, and they were gone.

The third wife approached and I heard them speak. Man and wife.

"Oh, wife, I have given you children. In our bed, we have created life that will live beyond our span. Will you go with me now where I must go?"

"Husband, you have given me seed and made of me a mother, but you have loved me only because you were fertile. I will not go with you, for I am no longer yours. Husband, you have not loved me except as you have loved a stranger, in a fogged mirror, a vessel at the well. I will go with you and bless you in the grave with a handful of dirt. There I must leave you. Beyond, I cannot go."

The third wife backed away and veiled her face, so that her eyes were dimmed behind the gauze of thin homespun.

Then came to the dying man his fourth wife. She was simply dressed. Unlike the other three, she looked him straight in the eye, and her own eyes were sad beyond sadness. Her eyes were as mirrors. Her eyes were as liquid silk. I heard them speak. Man and wife.

"Oh wife, I have forgotten you. I do not know your name. These others have I lived with, and bred with, and desired. Now they have refused me, and I ask with my last breath. Will you go with me now where I must go?"

The fourth wife spoke, "Oh, yes, husband, I will go with you. I will always be with you."

And the man gasped in joy. "Then, wife, bring me to our ending at last."

"Yes, my soul, I will, for I see in your eyes my own eyes. I see that you have at long last remembered me."

The man looked at her without regret. "I see you. I remember you. At long last I know."

"Yes," she whispered. "Yes."

And the fourth wife pulled the brazier of burning cloves down upon herself and her husband. The light yellow petaled sheets curled and crackled with flame upon his chest as she embraced him in the fire.

I watched as they were consumed, and I crossed the watered door as the rich house burned behind me. I wondered if I understood what I had seen. Remembrance is earthly and the forgotten never dies? I sought my Master to ask him of this lesson, but he was not at the crossroads.

I sought him in the village near the waterfall, and he was singing in the common house. He was singing about lust and caressing a woman, and the people were laughing and dancing around him. And the men were amazed by his voice, and the women were amazed by his virility. It is said he fathered a son that night, but by my memory, and in my telling, it was more than one, and a daughter he also fathered on that night.

We made our beds in tall grass that was soon to be mowed for the cattle, and when we awoke, I told my Master about the four wives and about the lesson of Remembering and Forgetting. I told my Master how the cruel rich man had been punished in justice.

But my Master shook his head. "Mourn him, tall brown one, mourn him."

I was confused.

My Master explained, "He is not a rich man or a poor man. He is every man."

My Master continued, "Every man has four wives. The first is his body. It must leave him at death, for a man is not his body. It is a vessel that cannot be filled when it has been emptied. It cannot follow us.

"The second wife is his riches. When a man dies, the diamond falls from his hand and awaits its next owner, it calls to its next owner. Treasure eagerly departs from us despite our fear of losing our riches. It cannot follow us.

"The third wife is his family. They will come to his grave and mourn, but they will not go with him. For family is immortal, it cannot go with the dead. Dead branches behind, new growth ahead. Family cannot go with us.

"But the fourth wife is always with us. She is the sum of us. She is who we truly are. We are not men. We are not woman. We are self. Our knowing and unknowing, our deeds, thoughts, and blessings, and our curses, omissions, and ignorance. She will go with us all. The fourth wife is the most faithful of all. Take care to remember this well."

And so I have, and so I have told this to you.

XV
A Parting

Closing the book was like waking up, afraid that a bad dream wasn't over.

The story of the man and his wives hit too close to home. Events in the tales and the circumstances of my last day on this fertile earth were bothersome: the brown one and little Ali, the lost sons and the stray dogs, the magic of my little Master's statement, "She loves you," my wife and the four wives; all the coincidences had me off balance.

When I woke up that Saturday morning, everything had felt settled. My little mental Daytimer was all filled in. Eat breakfast, kill some time while my wife packed up, watch her go, kill myself; everything was decided. There was a comfortable sealed wrapper around that fated day.

I felt a peace, almost a serenity I had never felt. The struggle was over, as if I had spent years wrestling with a monster and finally just let go. Failure is the ultimate soft mattress. Maybe I'm sounding typically over-dramatic. Maybe I'm over-mixing my metaphors. I don't mean to. The facts seemed clear. All the drama was finished. I didn't even expect any applause, but I did expect a final curtain and an end to all the little voices on stage.

The little purple book was rippling my little fatalistic pond. The parables were urging me to do something. I didn't have the energy left to change my path. Doomed artist melancholy doesn't mix well with carnival magic.

Ali interrupted my soliloquy. "Karma." First his voice was strong. Then it was soft beside me. "Karma."

I looked at him. He was so thin. And though he was coffee

brown, I suddenly realized that there was cream in his skin, a subtle paleness in the liquid of his life. We had made our little journey together. It was time to let things happen the way I had seen them happening.

"Yeah, Ali. Time for my karma to come true."

Ali shook his head. "Karma." He pointed at his heart with a delicate finger. "Karma." He pointed at my heart. His feather touch on my chest made me shiver. "Karma," he said.

I stood and stepped away from him.

There was a lamppost at the curb, and I leaned against it. I leaned against it like I was watchin' all the girls go by. I looked up the street and saw the Ryder van at my house. I had hoped it would be gone. My plan was for her to be gone by now, just gone.

I turned to Ali. He was sitting alone on the black metal bench. The purple book rested in his lap. His eyes were on me. They had been on me all morning, and now, at noon, I couldn't bear it much longer. "Go home, Ali."

Ali shook his head. "Master." He held the book out to me. "Master."

"No, Ali. I am not your Master."

He laughed at me. I know when someone is laughing at me. Ali laughed at me. He held the book up. "Master."

Of course, I had the story wrong. I had been thinking that as the tales paralleled my day, my life, that my role was the Master. Suddenly, I was laughing at me.

Ali joined in holding up the book. "Hah, hah, hah...Master. Master!"

In the first of the tales, the Master had found the young brown boy. I had found Ali. That made me the Master. In reality though, Ali had found me. I remembered it now.

The first time Ali and I met was a winter morning. I stood outside in a prairie wind and rubbed my face with my gloved hands. I had tried to rub my face away. My wife had told me the night before that she was going to start looking for another place to live.

When I lowered my hands, Ali had been there like a bird trapped in a green down-filled parka, a flutter under a pile of laundry. Only a circle of his face peeked out of the cinched hood. His eyes had looked hungry. I had given him the fateful doughnut. Ali had found me.

Ali was the Master.

I laughed again. "Hah, hah, hah...Master." I pointed at Ali. "Master?"

He held up the book of tales. "Master."

"So what now, Master? What do I do now?" We were right in front of Stram's Bar. A Beatles' song was slipping off the jukebox and into the street around us.

"I'm looking through you," sang John, or was it Paul? I used to know.

"What do I do now, Master?" I pointed at the tavern door. "A little Rubber Soul and some beer? Or..." I pointed at the moving van up the street. "...Or my life up the street? Which will it be?" I bowed to him, mocking the situation, mocking the "*Tales of the Master*," mocking him. Most of all I was mocking me, mocking myself for starting to see the story in that damned purple book as my own.

"Which will it be, Master?"

Ali stood up. A breeze could have picked him up like cottonwood seed. Once more my little Master spoke. "Choose."

"That simple, huh?" I wasn't mocking now. I was too tired to mock.

"Choose," he said.

John or Paul's voice came out of Stram's. "You're not the same."

"Choose."

I let go of the lamppost, a little surprised I could and still remain standing. Then, I surprised myself again by taking a step. That first step was followed by two hundred and twenty-two more. I was at my front door. It was open.

I stared in through the screen. A woman was there closing a box. The last box in the empty front room was closed. The woman turned towards me and we looked at each other through that ripped screen door.

"Come in." Her voice was kind.

I stepped into the room, and the screen slammed behind me. "I never did fix the spring on this thing."

It flashed across my mind that I could go to the garage and get the tools and finally repair that stupid door. It had always slammed. I had always meant to fix it. I had never gotten the tools. Maybe if I fixed it now, she would stay. No, that's why I couldn't fix it. She might stay.

"It's not important," she said.

"No, I guess not."

"This is the last box." She looked around at the empty room. "Thank you for coming back. I wanted to say goodbye."

I was angry when she said that, but I didn't show it. "Ali and I were... I was busy... I took a walk. I... I didn't want to say goodbye."

"I know this is hard. It's hard for me."

Who was this woman? That moment as I heard her speak, I did not know her. I knew her hair. It was brown as oiled oak, and it smelled like vanilla. I knew her eyes. They were hazel and gold, and they were gentle, even though they knew too much, too much about me. I knew her body. The tilt of her hip as she stood there working the corner of her lips with her tongue. She was ten feet away, and I knew her warmth and her anger, her dreams and disappointments, her tears and her shoes. I knew all that. But I didn't know who this woman was standing in front of me, closing a box and saying goodbye.

"Can I help you?" I said, pointing towards the box full of the final odds and ends, knickknacks and pack rat scraps. "I'll carry that."

She took a deep breath. She granted my final request. "Sure. Thanks." She stepped back from the box.

I picked it up. I was surprised by how heavy it was. She held the door for me as I carried it outside and up the ramp onto the truck. I put it down. The truck was two-thirds full. All of our stuff, refrigerator, tables, lamps, dishes, rugs, and a bed, and it was two-thirds full. Twenty years together and it was two-thirds full.

"I moved all your books into the den and bedroom so I'd have room to move," said the woman.

"Thank you." I am a polite man.

"I left you the futon and some other things you'll need."

"I don't need much."

She cracked a little. "Stop it. Stop disappearing. You always disappear." Then almost to herself, "It's so sad. I can't be sad anymore."

"I'm sorry."

She looked straight into my eyes, and I almost recognized her. "Yes, I know, you're sorry. I really do believe you are. I'm sorry, too."

I jumped down out of the cargo box, picked up the ramp, and slid it in under the bed. The steel rumbled and then clicked closed. I jumped to grab the overhead gate rope and it slammed down. I threw the locking lever and looked at her.

"Thank you." She was a polite person, too.

"Drive careful."

She walked around and climbed up into the driver's seat. The yellow door clattered when it slammed shut. The woman turned the key. The truck's engine was deep and real. The sound of it made my legs vibrate a little. I was standing so close.

She looked down at me. "You can call me. I left my new number by the kitchen phone."

"Sure."

She had her arm crooked out the window, just like a real truck driver. Her elbow was beautiful. "You can call me."

"Sure."

She couldn't help herself. "It wasn't all bad. So much of us was so good. I made some mistakes."

"I made most of the mistakes," I said.

Her head nodded, "Yes, yes, you made most of the mistakes. The deal is, I forgave you. I didn't forget, that's true, but I forgave you. Jesus! You just never let go of your own mistakes. You kept dragging them out like mummified cats or something. I forgave you for everything."

"Yes, you did," I agreed.

"Everything." she repeated. "You didn't kill her, Cole. You

couldn't save her. You're not God, Cole."

"No, I'm not God." I wanted to remember this woman's name. I couldn't.

Whoever she was, I think she was starting to cry. Her eyes were glistening. "I have to let go of it, Cole. If you can't... I can't be here anymore."

"Thank you for the forgiveness." I wanted to be invisible.

She put the truck in gear. "I guess I just got tired of being reminded of how much I had forgiven. Take care."

The gears ground a little when she slapped it into first. The truck shuddered a bit, then slipped out of the driveway into second gear, turning north towards the interstate. A block away I heard her hit third gear. Fourth gear was a smooth shift and a quick fade as the yellow truck crested the hill and magically slipped away.

Then I realized who she had been, and I cried. I cried in the empty driveway. I reached into the pocket of my sweater and grabbed the rounded stone from Doctor Finch's house. Tadesse had held it as he died. Now I screamed and threw it at her and the horizon. In my fury it slipped as I threw, and the stone skittered weakly into the street in front of the house.

I sat down on the asphalt and tried to rub my face away. There was a small brown hand on my shoulder. My little Master stood behind me.

"Master," Ali's voice was so quiet after the roar of the truck.

"No, Ali, I can't read anymore right now." I turned and looked at him. If he was my Master, like the tales suggested, now was the time for some answers.

"Ali, what did it mean? What did the 'Four Wives' mean? Okay, if you're the Master here, tell me!" The anger of it surprised me.

Ali didn't flinch. He just said, "Masters not always tell."

"Oh, that's great!" I was arguing with an eight-year-old who could barely speak English. "Do you know what I've done, Ali?"

Ali's eyes were calm. "I know. I know. Book. Master."

"Hah! Then tell me what to do, Ali. Tell me what you know."

Ali was more like a parrot. He didn't know.

"Master," said the boy.

"Yes, you're the Master. So tell me, Master, what did the tale mean? Did it mean I'm stuck here alone with my mistakes? What does all of this mean, Ali? Am I a lost son? Where is the magic? What lesson am I supposed to learn?" I was almost shouting at him.

A woman's voice stopped me. "Please! Please! The child... the child!" Ali's mother, wearing her long dark dress and white head scarf, ran towards us. "The child!" She seemed to catch herself for a moment. "My son! My son!"

She grabbed Ali before I could say a thing.

She was a stout woman. Not fat at all, but solid, like an elongated egg made out of walnut. Not ugly at all, just earthier than beauty. She swept Ali up in her arms, invisible in long sleeves. They went through their front door, and it slammed behind them. I was alone except for the little book laying in the patchy grass.

I picked up my tales and went inside my empty house.

XVI
The Tale of God's Foot

Our wanderings brought us to the Lake of No Further Shore.

There the waters stretched out to where the sun emerged from its depths. There the waves were as those of the sea. There were great white birds and long snouted fish that laid eggs. There, on its shore, was the city of gray granite walls and black wood halls.

At noon hour, we reached a hill that looked down on the city. My Master took off his robe and wrapped it around his head, for he had no hair to shade him. The day was gold.

Upon the sentinel hill we sat near the standing stone that had been raised by wise men of legend. And the standing stone was smooth on the lower part, where travelers and townspeople had leaned their backs against it year upon year. And the top portion of the stone was smooth, where the sky had leaned against it for year upon year. My back and my Master's back pulled in the warmth of it, and he spoke to me.

"Brown one, I am tired in my bones. Go into the city and get water for me. Your legs are young."

My legs ached with travel, also. For it is written that the hardest travel is down the mountain. But my Master had need of water. So my feet were called.

I answered my Master, "I will bring you water, Master."

He closed his eyes to the sun, and scratching his back against the holy standing stone, spoke to me again:

"Bring me water, and bring here to me the most valuable thing in the city.

Bring to me water for my mouth, and place before me the treasure of treasures of that city. We have come here to possess it. Go and do this for me."

The treasure of the city was unknown to me, for I was young, and new to this region. There were no stories of it that were held in my memory. But my Master had spoken and his eyes were closed to me.

I answered, "I will bring you this treasure. For that is what you ask."

Both sure and unsure, I went down to the walls. Even unsure, I would go because my Master had bid me.

The city gate of gray stone was guarded by men clad in iron leggings. Their helms were polished bronze. In their hands were mighty stone hammers, and their faces showed no welcome. And these men were six feet tall. The challenge was spoken, and their voices sounded as the growl from tethered lions.

They spoke, "You approach the city of Baga. What is your business?"

I answered as a young traveler, my hands empty and my eyes to the ground. "My Master sits by the stone. He has need of water."

With a sound like bending metal they bade me enter without welcome.

Said they, "Go no further than the well, brown one. Go no further than the well."

Within that gate of stone was a stepped pool, and many were drawing water there, for the hot part of the day was upon the city. There flowed the water, and by it stood a woman with yellow scarf and raven hair. On her bare shoulder was an enameled blue amphora, and as she moved, water splashed slightly from it, running as small rivers across her bare breasts and belly and dampening her white linen skirt. At her feet were three naked children, and their laughter was the laughter of the lake.

She spoke to me, "Young stranger, why do you grace us with your beauty? Few come unannounced to the city of Baga, and few have such mystery as you hold in your eyes. Why do you grace us at this well?"

In respect I replied, "My Master has need of water."

The woman gazed again upon me, and her voice was a welcome, "Our water is before you. But will you carry it in your mouth to him?"

Embarrassed by my stupidity, I told her more. "He also asks for the treasure of this city. The most valuable thing within this city I must bring to him."

The woman laughed, and the children laughed.

"You have no guile, young stranger. Will you steal our treasure and sing as you do so? You have announced it at the well, and the words spoken at the well flow like its water through the city. Your words will find every street, every alleyway, and every crack in every roof."

In my foolishness, and surrounded by her naked children, I laughed, too. In the sight of her breasts and belly damp with water, I laughed, and I repeated my foolishness.

"I will bring my Master his water and his treasure."

And then of a sudden the laughter was stilled, for she pulled me with her unencumbered hand. She pulled me to her and whispered as a conspirator.

"Do you not see the guards of our city? They are mighty men, and cruel, and the joy of the lake is dimmed by their watchfulness. Would you see that which they value most?"

I answered her in gratitude,

"I would see it, lady. Show this treasure to me."

And the woman waved her children away, and putting down the blue water jar, she bid me follow. Whereupon, we reached the second gate in the city. The second gate was copper, green in the wind of the lake. Before it stood men with ebony leggings. Their helms were of tortoise shell. In their hands they wielded long razors made of diamond, and their faces showed no welcome. And these men were seven feet tall. The challenge was spoken, and their voices were as the hiss of vipers in woven baskets.

They spoke, "You approach the second gate of Baga. What is your business?"

The woman spoke for us. "We are called to work. We must enter the place of making."

With a sound like rocks birthing rocks, they bade us enter without welcome.

Said they, "Make well and take nothing. We have word of your thieving, brown one. Make well and take nothing."

Within the second gate were workshops without number, dedicated to every skill of man. The woman showed them to me and taught me many things.

She taught me to soften leather and make a pack to hold and carry.

She taught me how to melt gold and form it into rings.

She taught me how to turn a wooden staff and give it the magic of the animals.

She taught me to weave and to sew, to shape the gifts of plants and beast.

She taught me all this and more, until, at last, we came to the third gate.

The third gate of the city was made of spider webs, to entangle the unwary. Before it stood men in suits of bone. Their helms were of leopard claw and emerald. In their hands were short swords, tempered in maiden's blood, sharpened and barbed, and their faces showed no welcome. And these men were eight feet tall. The challenge was spoken, and their voices were as the bear in a dry winter den.

They spoke, "You approach the third gate of Baga. What is your business?"

The woman spoke for us, "We are called by love. We must enter the place of pleasure."

With a sound like lightning striking water, they bade us enter without welcome.

Said they, "Make love while you may. But remember you, brown one, the fate of thieves is harsh here. Make love and take nothing."

Within the third gate was a fog and the sounds of passion. The sounds were full of little deaths. My eyes were filled by the woman's beauty, and for the first time, knew a woman as mate and more. In that circle of the city, a piece of life was mine that I had not had before. Her breasts and mine. Her belly and mine and sweetness in that circle of the city.

And we came to the treasure's gate.

The Treasure Gate was adamant and sulfur fire. Before it stood one man, covered in living scorpions. His helm was a crown of vultures, and he had seven heads and seven helms. His arms, like spiders, ended in spears made of whale ribs and tipped with spikes from the thorns of the long briar. And this man was nine feet tall. The challenge was spoken, and his voice was as a thousand bats in darkness.

He spoke, "Why would you see the treasure of Baga?"

And the woman answered for us, "We have drawn from the well of life. We have worked and drawn usefulness from the things of the earth. We have been man and woman together. Now, we are ready to see the treasure of Baga."

With a sound like a dying man's last rattle, he bade us enter without welcome.

Said he, "You may enter and you may emerge, but thieves remain in agony. Recall my words, brown one, as you behold the Foot of God. Take nothing!"

Within the Treasure Gate was a great round black wood table. Surrounding on the East, West, South, and North were the torches of worship. On that great black table there was another round black table, only smaller, and another and another and another and so on. Each was smaller than the one below it, and they were set upon one another so that we climbed them together.

On the second highest table sat a man in black robes. And his skin was black. And his eyes were black, and he wrote in a book he held.

And he wrote in black ink.

He said to us, "This is as high as you may go. For on the next table is the Foot of God. None may approach closer."

Looking up, I beheld this foot. The foot was of a man ten feet tall. It was large and the toes were painted, as the men paint their toes in that land. And the ankle had been cut so that the foot was there alone.

Though his eyes did not invite me, I put to him my question: "Tell me, good priest, what are you writing?"

And the black priest said, "I preserve the sayings of the famous, and ponder the subtleties of parables; I seek out the hidden meaning of proverbs and become more familiar to the Foot of God."

I asked the black priest, "Then does God limp, missing his foot?"

And the black priest wrote down my words but did not answer. He read my words, and he pondered, but he did not answer.

I asked the woman, "Is this the treasure these men most value?"

She answered, "It is the reason for the walls, the reason for the watchfulness. It is the secret thing. It is the Foot of God. This, they hold most dear."

Then, I did take her hand and we left the Treasure Gate where the guard did examine me. And the third gate where I was examined and the second gate where I was examined, and at last we reached the well. And by the well, the woman gave me her blue vessel full of water.

I thanked her and asked in my boldness, "What is your name, fair woman?"

And she gave to me her name, "My name is Farewell. For so, I say to you in love. And so by our love there shall be another child by this well."

And she named her children, "This babe is called Waiting, and she is growing."

The child kissed me upon the cheek and blessed me.

The woman spoke again, "This babe is called Hoping, and he is sweet."

The child kissed me on the hands and blessed me.

The woman spoke yet again, "This babe is called Lost, and she is my delight."

The child kissed me on the feet and blessed me.

The naked children laughed all around us, and the fair woman gave me an embrace. And she whispered the name of our child who was to come. And that babe would be called Truth.

I left in wholeness. And I took the water to my Master by the standing stone. One eye he opened, and he held me with that one eye. I waited for his words.

He gave them, "Have you brought me water, brown one?"

I told him, "Yes, Master, I have brought you water."

I handed my Master the blue amphora and taking it in his hands, he placed it to his dry lips and drained much of it. The water splashed on his cheeks and puddled around him in his carelessness. He drank deep as a man can.

When he had finished, he wiped his mouth with both hands and asked me, "And did you bring me the Foot of God?"

I admitted to my Master, "No, Master."

And he reproached me, "Why did you not bring the treasure of God's Foot to me?"

I told my Master, "It was of no value. You asked that I bring you the most valuable thing in the city, but what I found of great value there in Baga, I could not bring you."

My thoughts were of the woman within.

My Master asked me, "Did you meet the woman at the well?"

I told him, "Yes, Master."

My Master asked me, "Did you make love to her?"

I could not but smile, "Yes, Master."

And my Master smiled in his memory, "So did I so many years ago. Did she tell you her name?"

I answered him, "Yes, Master."

In anticipation he asked me, "What was her name?"

So I told my Master her name. "Master, her name was Farewell. That is the name she gave me."

My Master leapt to his feet and began dancing. He made sounds like a desert village celebration, and he held me in his arms as he danced in joyous abandon. As a mad man, he laughed and cried, and his eyes were full of tears and his mouth full of rejoicing. My Master was clapping his hands and hopping like a frog in warm mud when the winter ends.

And when his breath was used, he stopped and smiled at me as he rejoiced, "Her name was Farewell. You have brought me her name. She has at last given me her name, and it is Farewell. It is the sweetest of things, Farewell. The most valuable of things, Farewell. At last I have heard it, Farewell."

Then I asked him, "I have done as you asked, Master?"

"You have done as you were meant to do, brown one. Did you see her children?"

"Yes, Master. Their names are Waiting, Hoping, and Lost."

And my Master's smile was beyond a smile, "One of them is from me. When I was a Master, I made her, and her name is Waiting. And my Master before me made his part of Hoping, and his Master before is in the one known as Lost. Soon there will be another child by the fountain.

The child will be from you. And the cycle is complete in Truth."

And my Master held me and said, "You have given me the woman's name. Her name had been lost to me in my wanderings. That true name, that treasure, was eclipsed in my mind by the fear and the dangers of this world. As a storm can make a man forget the sky, as the flash of lightning brings blindness and not light, I forgot in my selfishness. I hoped to find that name again. For a true name is more than a name. A name is the whole of a thing. To lose that name is to lose a key, a key that would open a lifetime. Then I found you, brown one, and I sent you, in your innocence, to search. I was waiting for that treasure, for that key, for that freedom, and for that lifetime. I was waiting to hear her name. Her name is Farewell. That is the truth of all. Her name is Farewell, mother of truth. You have given me the wealth of this city. Take care to remember this."

And so I have, and so I have told this to you.

XVII
A Treasure

An empty house has an empty smell.

My house, I thought, smelled like God's Foot. The thought of what God's Foot smelled like made me laugh to myself. I was confused, frankly. Maybe I was on the verge of insanity, which, as a former friend had once told me, put me on the verge of sanity. Everything depends on your point of view, doesn't it?

My books were still there. She'd left me my computer, too. All my writing was on the hard drive, all of the words I'd stayed up late with, all the sentences I'd argued with, all the stories that had betrayed me. I touched the space bar, and the Mac woke up. I double clicked a folder on the desktop labeled "JPEGs." A formation of icons was revealed. I found the one I was looking for, and the image unfolded on the monitor.

The face was familiar. I had seen her driving a yellow truck out of my driveway not so very long ago. Her dark brunette hair was tied back with a leather strip. Her eyes were green in the vacation sun that struck her face. The olive skin of her bare shoulders was a rich brown from the sun, and the white shirt she wore was damp from the waterfall behind her. She was smiling. On the other side of the screen I was smiling, too. I had typed a caption beneath the image.

-Sophia-
a box of ocean
arrives from a far island
her breath is in it

Now, I remembered. Her name was Sophia. Now, I remembered the waterfall. I remembered the trip to Costa Rica. I remembered her skin. Soft as the rain in that forest. I remembered that we made love. I remembered we watched turtles on a beach, and I remembered that we made a baby. Her smell, her taste, her warm passion, her joy; it all came back to me. The fact and fantasy of her was overwhelming. She was Sophia. She was my wife. She was gone.

I went in the kitchen and there, next to the phone, was the message pad. She had left her new number just as she said she would. I could call her. I could beg her to come back. I could apologize again for everything I'd done and not done. Maybe one more "I'm sorry" would work. I picked up the phone.

I hung up the phone. My mouth was dry. I put my head under the kitchen sink faucet and let the cold water run through my hair. I drank straight from the nozzle. I picked up the phone. I hit the number one.

I hung up the phone. My mind was blank. What was I to say? I turned and looked for my little Master Ali, and then I remembered that he'd been taken home by his mother. This morning, I had been bothered when I first saw him. Now I needed him, and he was gone, too. But the little purple book was still there. *Tales of the Master* sat there on the floor where I'd put it down. Nothing was making a lot of sense in my head.

I picked up the phone. I'd call and leave a message. She couldn't be there yet. I'd wait for the beep and tell her I was sorry.

I hung up the phone.

I picked up the phone. I'd leave a charming and witty bit of a quip, and she'd love me again. If I had the right words, she'd love me again. I was a writer. All I had to do was find the right words.

I hung up the phone.

I picked up the phone. I'd recite the haiku I had written for her on that trip when I fell so much deeper in love with her. I knew I was in too much love the minute I started being afraid of losing her. When the baby came, I was beyond love. I ended up beyond hope.

I hung up the phone.

Were the words in the Oxford or in Roget's or in my head?

Then, I remembered I'd run out of words. Then, I remembered the struggle was over. Then I realized someone or something was scratching at my door. I crossed the bare front room and opened the screen door. To the side leaning against my house was Ali. He looked very weak.

Ali held the rounded stone in his hand, the stone from Finch's farm I had thrown in the street. Tadesse's stone. He reached out to give it to me, but his strength failed, and he slumped, dropping the stone as I caught him. It hit the step and rolled into the scraggly hedge by the stoop. Ali reached for it, and a small sigh escaped him.

"Stone," Ali murmured. "Stone."

"I'll get it later, Ali," I said as I picked him up. He felt like an empty envelope. He was too cold, even for early spring.

I brought him inside and sat him down on the lonely pillow by my writing desk. His eyes were the same as before, and that helped me. I brought my Master a glass of water. He drank it down in one or two quick gulps.

"Does your mother know you're here, Ali?" He'd climbed out of his window again. I'd seen him do it before.

He gave me a conspiratorial smile and a wink. I'd taught him how to wink at Georgia one morning when she gave us both doughnuts. It was a simple skill that he had grown very proud of.

"I should tell your mother you came back over here, Ali." I mean, I could try to tell her. His mother rarely spoke to strange men, even if they lived next door, even if they bought her son breakfast and dragged him all over town. I could go and try to explain to her. She wouldn't listen. She was forbidden by her culture from listening. And her husband, Big Ali, wasn't a tolerant man. I didn't want any trouble. I just wanted a quiet day.

Then Ali smiled at me. "Read."

"More of the silly book, Ali?"

"More silly. Read," he said.

I opened the book and looked for the words.

XVIII
The Apology Tale

In his joy, we walked. For my Master knew her name. I walked with my Master and his song. His singing met the air around us, and my ears heard musicians gathered in his throat.

> *I am in love with Farewell.*
> *My sandals are light in the going.*
> *Her name lingers like a sweet bell*
> *The river takes leaps as it's flowing.*
> *Farewell,*
> *to the lake and stone.*
> *Farewell,*
> *to my body's bone.*
> *Farewell.*

> *I live in freedom, Farewell.*
> *The journey is bright in the making.*
> *My path speaks but it doesn't tell.*
> *The seeking is finding not taking.*
> *Farewell,*
> *to the gate and hall.*
> *Farewell,*
> *to the pilgrim call.*
> *Farewell.*

His voice was as strong as a young man's, and his stride was as a soldier homeward bound in peace. And we followed as our feet found for us the way without thinking. The road was easy, and the day was warm to pleasing. And the day was bronze. Farms were to both left and right. Crops and pasture under the sky that prayed to our eyes as we gazed upon the scene.

The path became a road, became a king's highway, and there were many wagons and their drivers. The wine was loaded, and the grain. The goods were carried, and the ore and ingots. There were oxen, donkeys and horses at work, and my Master and I settled under a prophet's oak to let them pass. For late afternoon was upon us, and the inns began to fill as the road emptied of its burdens.

The heat of late day was upon us. I sat beside my Master, and we crossed our legs as we observed the empty roadway. It was not yet dusk when we would meditate, each in our own silence.

So I spoke to my Master. "I have never seen so many animals and wagons, Master."

He picked his teeth with a straw and nodded.

I spoke again, "There is so much manure upon the road."

"So much manure," he agreed.

"It would seem to be unclean and distasteful," I observed to my Master. The odor of so much manure was stronger than I had known from the quiet paths of my youthful days.

My Master sucked on the straw in his mouth and gave me a lesson.

"Manure is what it is. The horse eats his grain and shits it out. The ox eats his grass and chews it thrice and shits it out. The donkeys can shit without eating. Men can shit like donkeys. But it is not unclean, none of it is unclean. For the peasant knows to take that manure and dry it for his fires, to warm his family. The peasant follows the oxen and takes up their dung and fertilizes his crop to feed his family. The peasant gathers the horse manure, and the blossoms surround his house in profusion. For manure is life. Our mistakes are manure. Make of each what you choose."

Then my Master stood and walked to a pile of manure and took the straw from his mouth. He dipped its end into the manure and pulled out the straw. It was covered in dung.

Placing the straw in his mouth, he said, "It is good manure, it was a good mistake."

Then he spat the straw out upon the road and said, "But it is not for eating." My Master smiled.

I asked one more question that day. Pointing at the dung I said, "If the manure is mistakes that we can use in our lives, what then are the flies?"

The evening's biting flies were now becoming clouds around all the dung piles in the road.

My Master saw them and sitting down beside me he said, "The dung is our mistakes. The flies are our apologies. Those flies are more bothersome than useful. Take care to remember this."

And so I have, and so I have told this to you.

XIX
Three Visitors

The wisdom of the Tales had overcome my skepticism.

Or was I just too tired to think straight? I hadn't slept well for weeks. I was vulnerable to all sorts of crazy thoughts. Whether or not the book was true seemed unimportant to me. Whether or not Ali was my Master was too difficult to argue about with myself. In a lost corner of my head was a chance. The chance was small. The slightest rational thinking could kill it. I decided to stay a little crazy. I am a little crazy.

Ali was snuggled up with his head on my knee. He seemed comfortable now. The early afternoon breeze came in through the screen door. Ali's breath synchronized with it. I stroked his hair. When I thought he was asleep, I eased out from under him and settled his head on the pillow.

I went to the bathroom. Sophia had left me the Costa Rican beach towel, emblazoned with the words "Pura Vida," and the electric toothbrush. Had she cleaned out the medicine cabinet? I was scared. I opened the mirrored door. There was a bottle of Excedrin, a tube of toothpaste, and a jar of foot powder. Sophia had always hated the foot powder. She said that it made my feet smell like a veterinarian's office. I'd used the last of it months ago. Then, suitably rinsed, it had become the receptacle for my stash of Ativan. I'd been hoarding my pills for a couple years, one for me, one for the stash. There were enough pills there to do the job.

A knock at the front door stopped me from counting the pills yet again. Last week there had been sixty-seven of them. Two more knocks, this time louder, bounced around the empty house. The foot powder jar went back on the shelf. It relaxed me to know that the pills were there. Four knocks in quick succession sounded like a woodpecker on a car hood. Afraid Ali would wake up, I went to the door. I wasn't in the mood for visitors.

Standing there with her hair up in a tight bun, wearing a severe brown jacket and dress to mid-calf, was the reddest lipstick I had ever seen. As I half opened the door, she launched her perfume into my face. It was like a Woolworth's scent aisle had exploded in my face. A cloud of gardenias, roses, and funeral parlor orbited my nose.

The disorientation deepened as she spoke. "Good afternoon, sir. How are you today? My name is Marlene, and I want to talk to you about heaven."

A small tanned girl with beautiful green eyes and lustrous black Mediterranean hair peeked out shyly from behind the pale fat white woman with the cardinal-colored lips. She was like an apparition. Her voice was so familiar that it almost stopped my heart.

"I'm Hope!" She trilled. Was she talking to me or to the fat woman? "I'm Hope!" she repeated and whirled past the intruder. Hope came in the slightly opened door and clung to me. She and I both inside, looking out at the huge red lips.

Marlene – I remembered her name – went on, " I'm witnessing for Jesus Christ my Lord and Savior today. Do you have time to listen to his message?"

"I don't know. I..." I looked down at the girl. She was four, maybe five years old. About the same age as...

My visitor went on. "I have hope for you. Can you listen?"

The little girl transfixed me. Her eyes were taking in everything. They ate up the empty room behind me. The green eyes locked on Ali sleeping in the den beyond. There was another message here besides the one the woman carried in her worn black Bible.

It was obvious. "Come in, come in." I ushered her into the vacant space of the living room. The little girl clung to my leg, but her gaze was centered on the sleeping Ali, still within sight through the archway that separated the two small, nearly empty rooms. The big missionary was a bit surprised to be invited in, and then she was confused by the lack of furniture. The windows were without blinds or curtains, the walls white with an occasional bare nail punctuation. The floor was institutional blue-green berber carpet. It needed to be vacuumed.

She turned slowly in a circle scanning it, looking for a place to sit. She kept up her verbal stream. Silence, even the slightest pause, would make the vacuum of the room deadly.

"There was a time when I was frightened, sir. A time when my life was consumed by sin and uncertainty. But that time is past now. Is your life a happy one, sir?"

I paused just enough to unsettle her, and then I told her the truth. "No, my life is not a happy one. It's not happy at all."

That brightened her face. "Jesus can save you. His message is in this book. He has died for your sins, and He is coming back soon to make the whole world His."

"When is he coming?" I wanted to know. I really wanted to know.

"Soon, very soon now. Jesus will return, and his kingdom will be established." Her face was fleshy and certain. Her blue eyes were beautiful in their conviction.

"How soon?" I needed to know.

"Can we sit down and I'll.... " She trailed off as she remembered there was no place to sit, no rest in the room. Hope was shyly separating from my side. The girl was two arm lengths away from me, drifting towards the den with invisibly small steps. The woman looked at her with the same wonder in her eyes that I felt in my own. Hope was a series of still photographs, each image a micron closer to Ali.

I watched Hope, but spoke to the big woman. Marlene, that was her name. I remembered it again. "Marlene, it's very important that you tell me when Jesus is coming back. Is he coming back today?"

"Well, no. Probably not today. Certain things must come to pass before..."

"What things? Let's do them now. Can we do them? Is there

any chance at all it could be today? Tomorrow morning at the latest? You see, I'm going to kill myself tonight, and that might be a mistake if Jesus is coming back. I could hold out for a few days maybe, but I need to know." It just flooded out of me without thinking. All of it was said matter-of-factly, as if I was talking about my vacation plans, which of course, in a sense I was. "What exactly has to happen so that he'll come back? Can we hurry him up at all?"

She was thinking hard now. She wasn't sure she'd heard me correctly. After all, no one just tells a stranger that they're going to kill themselves. Not in the first minute of their acquaintance. Marlene looked towards Hope. The little girl had settled on her knees, two feet from Ali's head. It almost looked like a Holy Card. The sunlight through the west-facing den window and the dust of a recently plundered house almost gave the two children halos. Marlene was focused on Hope.

"Is the boy yours, too?"

I wasn't sure what she meant by that. "No, the boy is my neighbor."

"They are lovely children."

"Yes, they are." It was a lovely little vision in my den.

Marlene was quiet, taking in the sight of the children. Her big over-made-up face was enraptured.

So was I, in more ways than one. I broke the spell. "When is Jesus coming, Marlene? I need to know."

Marlene's round head turned back to me. Her spiel had been disrupted. But true faith always triumphs, and a flame soon appeared above her head. The Holy Spirit was upon her again.

"Pray with me," she said, and one of her meaty hands grabbed my shirt and tugged.

She was a strong woman. Strong in her devotion and strong in her right arm. When she tugged, I teetered. Marlene trusted in her God to save her, and she let her knees buckle. The force of her maneuver could not be resisted by a mere human such as I. Laws of physics had to be obeyed. Marlene was heading down, and my legs had to follow or snap. For a heartbeat, we were weightless as we hung in midair. Then gravity, mass, and momentum took over from inertia. The two of us hit the floor with our knees, and the house shook like a propane tank had exploded out back.

Ali snapped to a sitting position. His eyes widened when he saw Hope kneeling in front of him. Adoration ruled her five-year-old face.

"The stone!" said Ali. "The stone!"

"I'll get it later, Ali. I'll get it later."

"The stone!" He repeated. He was talking to me, but he was as mesmerized as I was by the little girl. He stared at Hope and yelled at me, "The stone!"

"Okay, Ali. I'll get the stone." It was important to him. I started to get up, but Marlene jerked me back.

"Pray with me." Marlene's kneecaps would hurt later – I was sure of it. But now she plunged ahead in her fervor. "Oh, Father, we ask in Jesus' name..." She tugged at my hand. She was prompting me.

I joined in. "...in Jesus' name..."

"That your lost child..." she continued.

"That your lost child..." My voice quavered with those words. But I was afraid to thwart her now. Besides....

"...could be brought to your bosom..."

I glanced at her bosom. Impressively generous it was. A tug, I caught up. "...could be brought to your bosom...."

Ali shouted from the other room. "Bosom! Bosom!" He laughed.

Hope joined in. "Bosom!" She giggled.

Marlene was unperturbed. "...and suckled by your grace..."

Disturbing images flashed through my mind. "...and suckled by your grace..."

"Bosom!" Hope and Ali cried in unison.

"Find comfort in the milk of your message..." Marlene's eyes were closed in prayer and concentration, which was good. God knows what she might have done if she had seen me smirk at that point.

"Milk of your message?" I did put a bit of a questioning lilt to that phrase.

"And the sweet cream of your redemption..." No doubt about it, Marlene was winging it totally.

"Bosom! Bosom!" Ali and Hope were dancing in a circle, holding hands and chanting, "Bosom! Bosom!"

I wondered about the pervasive influence of the dairy industry in Marlene's creed. "...the sweet cream of your redemption." If she mentioned Redi-Whip I was going to lose it.

Inspiration took her over the edge into ecstasy. "Bring him into thy embrace and let him enter into the land of milk and honey..."

"Bring me into thy embrace and suffocate me in thy huge bosom." I couldn't help myself.

Ali and Hope squealed in delight. "Bosom! Bosom!"

Marlene was not amused. She elbowed me with some authority, and I toppled off my knees like a ten pin on keg night at the bowling alley.

"Bosom!" I shouted, and I would have spurted milk out of my nose if I had been lucky enough to have a mouthful at that moment. I laughed like an eight-year-old.

The children laughed like children. "Bosom! Bosom!" The word had lost its meaning, but that only made it funnier.

Marlene was not amused. Her lip curled in disgust, and she scrambled off her knees. Meaning to stand in a huff, she lost her balance mid-huff and flopped on her side.

"Bosom!" shouted the kids, including me.

Marlene whimpered, tried to stand, and then like a miracle, she laughed. "Ah, hell," she said, and she laughed. She had a beautiful laugh that came from deep inside her. You could get pretty deep inside Marlene. "Ah, hell," she said again.

The rest of us joined in, "Bosom! Ah, hell! Bosom! Ah, hell!"

Marlene was flat on her back.

"You okay, Marlene?" I managed to get a sentence out.

She was out of breath from the merriment. "Yeah, I'm all right. I'm all right, but I can't get up." She laughed at herself. It was lovely. I'm not being sarcastic, she was lovely.

I made it to my feet and offered her my hand. "Let me help."

Marlene reached up and accepted my assistance. Bracing myself with my legs, she was soon vertical again. She straightened her little jacket and her dress, tugged at her pantyhose, and adjusted her bra straps. "Thank you."

Ali and Hope had stopped dancing about, and together they sensed the problem and wheeled the only chair in the house over to us. It was the office chair I used at my computer desk. Marlene looked at it, and then looked at me. I knew what she was thinking.

She wasn't embarrassed to say it. "If I sit in it, I'll be wearing it when I get up."

She was right. The width of the chair between the padded arms was not sufficient to allow her womanly figure easy egress once seated in its upholstered vise.

"I'll pry it off you later. Sit down."

"Thank you," said Marlene. She needed to take a load off, and so she did. She put her load in my chair. It squeaked...creaked...and it held. "Thank you."

"You're welcome." I was smiling, and so was she.

The children came and sat at her feet. I got her a glass of water. Marlene was a little out of breath from our little comedy revival scene.

"Thank you," she said. She sipped on the glass and eyed me, one eyebrow a bit higher than the other. "You really gonna kill yourself?"

"That's the plan." Thinking about that decision took away some of the fun of the moment. I saw no reason not to tell her the truth.

"What's your name?" Now she was getting personal.

"Cole."

"Why do you want to kill yourself, Cole?" Marlene leaned forward as far as her body and the tight chair would let her. I stood there like a grad student taking his orals. Then, I realized Marlene wasn't judging me at all.

I answered, "I thought I wanted to kill myself because I'm a failure, because my wife left me, because of all the mistakes I've made..."

"What mistakes have you made?" Marlene asked.

"Name it. I've made all the selfish mistakes a man can make." I looked at Hope when I said that.

"Did you repent?" The word didn't sound so Holy Roller the way she said it.

"I said I was sorry a million times, Marlene. I said I was sorry, and then I said I was sorry for saying I was sorry, and then I was sorry for being sorry. Oh, I have apologized, and I still owe so many more apologies!" The happiness was gone, and my eyes were filling with tears. Marlene was listening. Hope was listening. Ali?

Ali was at the screen door. He opened it just a crack. A buzzing entered the room. A black fly on the afternoon air turned right and left and circled and swooped and climbed on its invisible wings. This way and that and over and under and onto my hand. The black fly landed and sat there. The insect's eyes had as many lenses as I had apologies.

The tale had landed on my hand.

Ali brought me the book.

I asked our guests to stay. "Marlene, can I read you a story? Can I read Hope a story?"

She looked down at her bible in the middle of the floor where it had dropped when she fell. She looked at the purple book in my hand.

"You don't need my permission to read Hope a story. That's silly." The fat woman laughed. I was missing something, but she just went on. "Sure, read us a story." I liked her voice. "Read us a story, Cole." She had remembered my name. That was unusual.

Ali spoke softly, "A story for the stone."

So, Marlene and Hope and my little Master listened.

The house was not as empty as it had been.

XX
The Naked Tale

The sun set. Cows were taken back to their pens by farmers with worried eyes. And the dusk was orange.

My Master spoke to me as we walked. Even as the day darkened, we walked, because the journey had not decided to pause at that hour.

My Master spoke: "You have a fine robe, brown one. Does it make you happy?"

I answered, "Yes, Master. My mother wove it for me, and it makes me happy."

My Master walked on and said, "Then take off your robe, and drop it in the dust. Let it be behind you as we walk."

I removed my robe and we walked on.

My Master spoke again. "You have a fine pair of sandals, brown one. Do they make you happy?"

Walking without my robe, I answered him.

"Yes, Master. My father made them for me, and they are a joy to me."

My Master quickened his pace and he bid me, "Then kick off your sandals quickly, and stay at my side."

I kicked off my sandals and felt the warm dust of the road with my bare feet.

My Master spoke again. "That pack you carry is wondrously worked. Does it make you happy?"

I answered, "Yes, Master, for Farewell made it for me on the way to the Foot of God."

My Master, never slackening his pace, said, "Then give it to me."

I gave my Master my fine pack.

My Master spoke again, and as he spoke, he began to run. "Do not fall behind, brown one. Your loin cloth is fine linen. Does it make you happy?"

I ran as he ran, and I told him, "Yes, Master. For my sister spun the thread for it. It makes me happy."

Running even quicker he said, "Then take off your loin cloth immediately, and run with me."

As I ran, my hands unwound the cloth, and I was naked, and we ran. My Master and I ran. We ran side by side, and we ran until the smiling moon was high. And when the smiling moon was high, my Master stopped.

He examined me in my nakedness.

"Are you happy?"

In truth I told him, "Yes, Master. I am happy because I am with you."

He smiled. He laughed. And my Master told me, "Then go back and get your loin cloth, at least. Do you not realize that you are naked?"

I joined him in laughter, for I was naked.

"Yes, Master."

And my Master said, "Take care to remember why you are happy. Take care to remember this."

And so I have, and so I have told this to you.

XXI
Appearances

Little kids think the word "naked" is funny.

Ali and Hope loved the story of the nude traveler. They had giggled as each item of clothing hit the ground.

My little black-haired pal asked me a question. "Happy?"

I had to think about that. "I don't know, Ali."

Hope almost accused me. "You laughed like you're happy." Her voice was light but not as childlike as you might expect.

My eyes had to leave Hope. There was too much innocence on her face. And her eyes held more memories than they should have. Looking at Marlene, I answered, "You can laugh when you are sad. You can cry when you are happy."

"You act pretty happy for a man who's going to kill himself." Marlene looked at me with some amusement herself. Her eyes were so blue. Eyes were very important to me that day.

"Maybe Jesus has saved me, Marlene."

"Bring me some more water to wash the taste of that bullshit out of my mouth." She shifted a bit in the chair, and it groaned under her.

The kids went with that one. "Bullshit!" They rolled on the floor. "Bullshit!"

"I'm a little confused..."

The fat woman interrupted me. "That's an understatement, little man." All her sympathy for me seemed to have evaporated.

"Wait, you came in here with a Bible and a prayer about milk, cream, and bosoms."

"Bosoms! Naked! Bullshit!" The kids were in foul language heaven.

"Hope, honey, hand me my Bible, would you please?"

Marlene took her black book from the little girl's hand and

opened it. "My, she is polite. Thank you, dear." Marlene's relationship with Hope was different from most mothers and daughters I had seen. It was kind, but it seemed a bit distant.

Marlene turned to me. "Cole, the tale you read us is in here, too." She thumped the Bible page in her lap.

"Jesus never gets naked. That wouldn't go over well," I said.

"Naked Jesus! Naked Jesus!" shouted the children.

Marlene ignored us all. "Just listen. 'Sell all that you own and distribute the money to the poor. And you will have treasure in heaven. Then come follow me.' Don't you see, it's the same story? Give up the stuff you think you need to be happy so that you can find your treasure in heaven, your true happiness."

She was right. I had to give her that. "You're fat, Marlene." The words just popped out. Maybe it was my way of stopping the conversation. I could be cruel when I needed to be.

Marlene just laughed. "Yes, I am. I am fat. And tomorrow you'll be dead."

I wouldn't be distracted. "Have you always been a fat woman?"

Hope slapped me in the face.

"Hope! Stop that! Hitting is wrong! Good girls don't hit!" Marlene's voice was not sincere. The discipline sounded more like approval. She smiled at the little girl and stroked her black curly hair. "I know it's not my place, but..."

"Never mind." I said.

Ali walked over and touched my cheek. The stinging was sweet and alive.

Marlene chose to answer my earlier question. "Yes, I have always been fat. I will probably always be fat. I haven't always been happy, but I am happy now. I am happy today. I have Jesus, and I have my Bible."

I asked her, "Your Bible makes you happy?"

She laughed. It was obvious where I was going with this.

"Yes, my Bible makes me happy."

"Then give it to me." I held out my hand.

Marlene handed it to me without the slightest hesitation.

I asked her another question. "Does Jesus make you happy?"

"No." She surprised me.

"No?"

"No. But being with him makes me happy." She had that certain look again. Hope nestled up next to me again.

The moral of the tale seemed clear to me now. "So he is your Master? Just like in the story?" I held up my book, the little purple book.

She laughed again. "You really don't see it, do you?"

"Tell me." I really did want to know.

Marlene rubbed her hands together, thinking.

"Tell me," I insisted.

"I'm a Christian now, but I haven't always been. For awhile, I was Wiccan."

"You're a witch!"

Hope jumped up at that, and I pulled back like a dog on a gravel road. I didn't want to get hit again, even by a five-year-old, especially this five-year-old. My jaw still hurt from her first blow.

Marlene pulled the girl away from me gently. "No, not a witch. Kind of a pagan. The beauty of nature. The power of the earth itself. Wicca celebrates the natural state but..."

"But what?"

"It's missing the final step. Or, maybe I should say, it's missing the next step.

"What do you mean, the next step?" This fat woman was, pardon the expression, growing in importance to me.

"Nature is only part of reality. I think there's something beyond it." She had closed her beautiful blue eyes. She was like a female Buddha.

As if my thought had revealed itself to her, she continued, "I used to be Buddhist."

"Was that missing something?"

"No. Buddhism wasn't missing anything. That is, it was missing everything. That made it so full."

I jumped on that. "Buddhism was full of emptiness?"

She smiled. "Yes, but that was the beauty of it. It wasn't missing anything, because it wasn't trying to be everything."

"Heavy," I said with my best old hippie intonation.

She made eye contact at that. "Heavy, indeed."

"So, Buddhism wasn't missing anything. Then, why did you abandon it?"

"Because I was missing something," she sighed.

"What were you missing?" I was boring in on the core now. I felt like we were close to something here.

"I was... you'll misunderstand this." She was backing away.

"Don't be silly. I'm a writer. Writers never misunderstand."

She locked her blue eyes on me and smiled the biggest white teeth smile I'd ever seen. I noticed how white her teeth were. They looked like rounded perfect ivory eggs. There was a pause. I was amazed by the silence.

And then she said, simply, "Bullshit!"

There was another silence. It lasted two seconds. Then the empty house was filled with delirious laughter, gales of laughter, squeals of delight, chortles, guffaws, belly laughs - Marlene's belly laugh was earth shaking - howls and giggles.

"Bullshit!"

When it died out Marlene got herself together. She adjusted her bra straps again and asked me, "What makes you happy?"

I was on to her. "Nothing. Nothing makes me happy. I'm going to kill myself, remember?"

She wasn't going to let me off that easy. "Like I said, you act pretty happy for a man who's going to kill himself."

"Happy? I don't think..."

"What makes you happy, little man? You laugh. You flirt..."

"I flirt? I haven't been flirting with you."

"You think my eyes are beautiful."

"I never said..."

"Ah, but you looked at them like they were beautiful. Do you think I haven't noticed?" She was smiling. She was beautiful. "You ask me intimate questions."

"Intimate?"

"Yes, intimate questions about my body. Like, have you always been fat?"

"I didn't mean..."

"You laugh. You flirt. You seem very alive. You seem happy. But you're going to commit suicide, so what makes you happy?"

The answer hit me. Once again, for a reason I didn't understand, I revealed something so private to this fat beautiful woman I had known for one short hour. "I am happy because I have decided to die, because I am not debating the decision in my head, because for the first time in months, maybe years my head is quiet inside." Ali squeezed my hand. I hadn't even realized he was holding it. I looked at him. He was pale brown. His hand was cool in mine. "And maybe I'm happy because I've found my Master."

Marlene snorted. "You think he's your Master?"

"I guess I do, yes."

"Then you're missing something."

"What am I missing?" I looked at her. Maybe she could talk me out of this growing feeling that the purple book, the volume of *Tales of the Master*, was taking over my life. Maybe this Christian woman could snap me back to reality. "Tell me what I'm missing." It was a demand.

She hesitated. She was close to it again. Then, "I don't know. Maybe both of us are missing something. Maybe Ali is your Master. I don't know."

"I don't know, either. I was hoping..."

Marlene leaned towards me again. "If you are going to kill yourself, then what makes you happy?"

It hit me, "The pills...the pills make me happy. I have the pills to kill myself. I have them." I got up off the floor and headed to the bathroom, still talking. I pulled the foot powder jar out of the medicine chest. I brought them to her.

"See? I have the pills, and that makes me happy. I'm going to die, and it's not a fantasy, because I have the pills!"

She spoke very deliberately, and her teeth were very white as she smiled. "The pills make you happy?"

"Yes." I clutched the jar next to my chest protectively.

She sighed a fat woman's sigh. "Then give them to me."

It was weird. I didn't hesitate. I handed Marlene the pills.

"Now, read us another story."

I sat down cross-legged on the floor.

XXII
The Tale of
One Year with the Master

For one year, I walked beside the Master, and he did not speak.

We walked past farms and waded in the soft silt marshes. And the day was rose. We cut our hands on the flint rocks of Eden. My Master led me across the ash plains of Zagrefia. I bore his weightless body through the flood of Indusia. Our food was meager, and our food was mean. There were few people to bless our eyes in that year. Under sun and moon we traveled, and he did not speak.

We made no beds nor sat at any tables. We counted neither our steps, nor our wounds. My Master and I wandered the empty world where villages had not held, where clans and nations had not raised their voices. The wild animals were our court. The beasts were our judges. The birds were our generals. For one year we walked, and my Master did not speak. Then, after the thirteenth frowning moon, a crow cried stop, and so we stopped. The crow had told us, and we stopped.

I could not have taken one more step or moved another foot. My eyes were heavy with the year. My dry voice came forth then. For in that year, I had thought of many questions. They were questions for my Master, and I remembered that he was my Master and that it was my place to question him and learn. Despite my fatigue, I questioned him. Despite my weariness, I would ask knowledge of him. Undeterred by my exhaustion, I would seek from him answers.

"Master, when is the day we reach the end of this journey?"

My Master asked in response, "Where are we going?"

"I do not know," I answered.

My Master smiled and said, "Then perhaps we are here."

I laughed when I heard his words. And my Master laughed with me.

I asked him, "Then are we here?"

"A fool can ask more questions in a minute than twelve wise men can answer in an hour," he said through his laughter. "Here we are, and here we have always been. Take care to remember this."

And so I have, and so I have told this to you.

XXIII
A Puzzle

Confusion is a good state to visit.

A friend told me that once. He's dead now. He said that when you were confused, you were forced to take a new look at things. Actually he said, "If your head is up your ass, at least your ears are warm." I miss him.

I closed the book after reading the "One Year Tale" to my growing group of disciples.

"That's a nice story," said Marlene. I was starting to forget she was fat.

"Sleep," said Ali. He did look tired. My little Master had walked quite a distance today.

Hope stroked Ali's hair. There was something mystical about the way the two children related to one another, and something else I couldn't put my finger on. I'd had that deja vu feeling since Marlene and Hope showed up at my door.

"But what does it mean? What does the story mean?" I asked.

Marlene laughed again. "You really don't get it, do you?"

Hope chimed in, "Don't get it."

Ali smiled.

"Okay, so I don't get it. I suppose you do?"

"That's another question. You're asking more questions in a minute than twelve wise men could answer in an hour." Marlene was going to drive me crazy.

"Don't you have any questions? Am I the only one wondering what's going on here?" The situation was absurd. Of course, I was asking questions. What was I supposed to do? Was the book guiding me? If so, what was I supposed to think? How could I figure things out if I didn't ask questions? Who has time to take a nap when you're going to kill yourself? Was I asking too many questions inside my head? Did I think everything had to be questioned? Why was all this happening? Why did the birds go on singing?

"My, my," Marlene shook her head. "You've got a lot of questions don't you?"

I jumped on the opening. "You just asked a question."

"I did?"

"That's another question." I had her now.

"So it is. So it is." Marlene adjusted her bra straps again, leaned forward in the desk chair and tried to stand up. Sure enough, the chair had clamped on to her.

Hope, Ali, and I stood up to help her. The three of us together pried the monster off her ass, as round and fertile as a stone age Venus statuette. With great dignity, Marlene walked over to my desk. She was majestic.

Marlene picked up the rolled canvas I had retrieved from Doctor Finch's house. Opening it like a holy parchment, she looked at the portrait. The flapping hands, the protruding tongue, the clown's nose, and the frosting covered rooster made her smile. She turned the canvas over. There was something written on the back. I hadn't noticed it before.

She read it out loud. "I found this book, and it changed my life. There is no simpler way to face the truth of it. My ways were those of a lost man. In my mind, I was the center of everything. This small book showed me the truth of things. Now, there are a million masters. Dr. Ethon H. Finch, 1955." She looked at me. "Who's this Finch guy?"

Ali, Hope, and I in unison shouted, "Question! ...Question!"

"Knock it off." Marlene was serious now. "The point of the story was that you are where you need to be. Here and now, things are exactly what they are supposed to be. If you are a fool, you are a fool. And you, my friend, are a fool. But that's okay."

"That doesn't make sense." I had no idea what she meant.

"Okay. Simply this." She held up the foot powder jar, my pills - my suicide pills. I'd forgotten that I had given them to her. "The tale says to stop worrying about the situation you find yourself in. You are where you are. Now, who is this Doctor Finch?"

"He was the guy who wrote *Tales of the Master*."

"What makes you think he wrote it? It says on the back of the painting that he found it."

"That's all part of the scam."

"You're a suspicious guy, aren't you?"

She had me there. "You have no idea how suspicious I can be."

Marlene gave me the fat lady eye. "That's one of the reasons your wife left you, isn't it? You were suspicious of her."

"How would you know?" I was pissed that she'd pry into my private life. I mean, talking about suicide was one thing, but talking about my marriage was another thing altogether.

"Let me guess. You felt so unworthy of her. You figured she must be perfect. You were suspicious of why she stayed with you. Then you did something, something... whatever, and it just proved to you how unworthy you were. So you drove her away and confirmed your suspicions. You sad, pathetic little wimp."

She was right. I had to agree with her. "Yes, Marlene, I didn't deserve her."

"Oh, shut up! Of course you deserved her! You are so wrapped up in self-pity. It's very conceited. You thought she could do better. That way you were free to wallow around in the pleasure of despair. And now this little book cannot offer you anything, because it was written by a fraud and you see through it all." Marlene was bearing in now.

"Wait..."

"No, you wait. You are a self-indulgent, conceited, self-centered, condescending asshole. Poor you! You can wrap yourself up in tragedy and cynicism, and nothing can get through to you because you are so undeserving." Marlene was a mountain of irritation.

This was getting uncomfortable. I felt naked in front of her.

"Yes, you're right." I sighed, my shoulders slumped.

She whacked me on the back and nearly knocked the wind out of me. "Oh, stop it! You're trying to disappear. Something makes you uncomfortable, and you mumble and moan and try to disappear. Stop agreeing! Argue a little! Stop being so sure of yourself!"

Now I was confused. "How in the name of God am I sure of myself?"

"You're sure you're a wasted human being! The worst of the worst. God, you are conceited!" Marlene looked like she might hit me again.

"Help! Help!" Hope was screaming.

We turned and saw her standing next to Ali, trying to hold him up. His eyes were rolling back in his head. Hope was too small to support Ali when he collapsed. His little body fell, and he was face down on the floor. My Master had fallen.

Marlene moved faster than I did. She was to him in a heartbeat, and she gathered him in like a mother. She held him to her breast and stroked his head. "There, there, little boy. You're okay now."

I reached out and touched Ali's forehead. It was clammy, too cold again. "What's wrong with him?"

"I don't know," said Marlene. "Don't you?"

"I just let him tag along with me. He lives next door. I don't know... I really don't know." The helplessness was too familiar. Was it happening again?

"Let's take him home. Is his mom home?"

"Yeah. Yes, his mom is always home."

Marlene picked up Hope, too, and cradling a child in each arm, went out the front door. I hurried to keep up. We got to Ali's house, and I knocked. I knocked really hard, and I rang the bell, and I knocked on the heavy oak door.

The door opened slowly, and two eyes peeked around it from the dark room beyond. Then the eyes widened as they saw Ali lolling in Marlene's arms. The door swung wide, and Ali's mother rushed to him.

"My son! My son! Give him to me, please. Give him to me!"

She was grabbing at the boy, and Marlene gave him over.

I tried to explain, "He just passed out. We took a walk and..."

Ali's mother didn't even look at me. She took Ali, and as she disappeared back into the house, he looked at me over her shoulder. Ali smiled. My little Master smiled. Then his eyes closed.

The door slammed shut.

I just stood there.

"He'll be fine," said Marlene.

I turned to her. "What do I do now?"

"Oh, you poor thing. You're not worried about Ali. You're worried about you."

She was right, and it hurt.

Marlene, still holding Hope, who was trying to see through the walls of Ali's house, grabbed me with her free hand and tugged me back away from the porch.

I was frantic. "I've got to do something."

Marlene just looked at me with those eyes. "You're not God, Cole."

I'd already heard that once before, today. "No, I'm not." I didn't want that to be true. I wanted to be God and make everything past, present, and future okay.

Hope crawled from Marlene's arms into mine. "It's all right. It's all right." Her tiny body warmed me.

Marlene gave me a little push. "Come on, Cole. Let his mother take care of him. Let's go read the next story."

I let Marlene be my Master.

XXIV
The Tale of the Forest

The sun seemed to stop on that day, and a long path was ahead of us, and the day was vermilion.

A crooked path was before us, and it wandered as a lost ant up the steepness of the mountain. Our legs became weary. They were as stone. Through that day, my Master struggled with the path. For though he had the heart of youth, he had the legs of old men. Even as the sun did not move, and the peak of the mountain seemed to grow higher before us, my own legs became weights of iron, and my heart became a straining rope pulled ever tighter by a load of many bricks. That endless day we ascended, breath by breath, and toe by toe.

The summit between two summits was finally ten steps above us when my Master stopped. Upon that last turn in the path, he did stop, and upon the last switch of the trail, he did sit down in the dust of it. He did not have another step of his stride remaining.

And my legs carried me that last measure, so that I stood atop the slope. My eyes looked down from that high place and beheld the land beyond. It was a great forest that stretched away under my feet. A land of trees that was as an ocean of gentle green from the mountain past my reckoning to the edge of the earth as it was revealed. And I told my Master of the wonder before me. And at last my heart was light, and the sun did spin again as the day took up its heavenly way.

Then my Master spoke and bade me, "Brown one, you see beneath you the Forest of a Thousand Thousand Years. Long have I sought to hold it in my hand. Go and bring it. Go into that forest, gather it together, and bring to me all of it. Place it in my hand."

And because my Master asked it, my legs brought me down into the forest. My feet sought its center, and I followed them. My eyes beheld the branches and the twigs, the leaves and the acorns, the shadow and the light. I tasted of its berries and mushrooms, bitter roots, and sweet honey.

I listened to the forest breathing, and I listened to it sing in the wind like a harpist's quiet fingers. My nose brought the musk of its dwellers from burrow and den, from antler and lodge. My skin touched the forest by thicket and bramble, by tendril moss and thorn. My blood was upon the forest, and its life was upon me, so that we became one. I slept upon the wooded breast and dreamt of the milk within.

And when the time was full, I returned to my Master. Across that peak and ten steps to my Master.

My Master's head was bowed, and his lungs were still not full. He did not stand to greet me and spoke beneath that high wind in that high place.

"Have you brought me the Forest of a Thousand Thousand Years? Will you place it now in my hand?"

I approached my Master. I knelt at his feet. I bowed before him and brought my head down to rest on his hand. My Master held my head on his hand. And the day ended in that moment, and stars ruled the mountain sky.

Holding my head, my Master bent and whispered in my ear. "I chose well. For you have placed the forest before me."

My Master stroked my head and then made to me another bidding. "Now go into the Forest of a Thousand Thousand Years and bring back to me the most perfect leaf within that land.

Give into my hand from your hand the leaf I request."

My living feet did obey, and into the forest I searched for the most perfect of leaves. I searched near stream and high in the crowns of ancient trees. I examined leaves at the heart of the Morning Star Bush and leaves on the stalks of the Deep Woman Flower.

After many days, I rested in exhaustion, and before my face, the leaf of a Seven Dead Tree drifted into my lap as if it had been called to me. That leaf I took to my Master. From my hand into his I gave that leaf unto him.

My Master looked at the leaf. First one side and then the other side of the leaf he pondered. And then he spoke to me in the voice of kindness.

"You have failed, brown one. This is not the most perfect of leaves. You have failed."

With those words he tore the leaf in half. My Master placed half in his mouth and offered the other half to my tongue. We chewed the leaf in silence and the taste was bitter.

And my Master said to me, "You have failed, brown one."

I replied to him, "Pardon my failure, Master."

And my Master smiled upon me and spoke to me in kindness.

"No pardon is required. You have failed. It is a good thing to fail. I cannot praise you enough for your failure. To find the most perfect of leaves in that eternity of leaves would have made you a god. I rejoice in your failure. Gods are not good company for men, for gods trouble the roads, and when they stretch their legs, lands disappear. I would walk with you, brown one. I would walk with you and be glad you are not a god."

And my Master chewed the leaf. And I chewed the leaf. And the taste of this failure was sweet.

My Master spoke, "Savor the flavor of this lesson, brown one. And walk with me. Take care to remember this."

And so I have, and so I have told this to you.

XXV
A Need

Sometimes I need something so bad I forget what I need.

I needed to see Ali. I was totally caught up in this "master" fantasy. At least, that day, that moment, it still was more comfortable to think of it as a fantasy. To admit it was anything else would have meant that I was caught up in something out of my control.

I had read the "Forest Tale" to Marlene and Hope hurriedly, not even listening to my own voice as the words passed over my tongue. God, I was even beginning to think in the archaic phrases of the book.

Marlene spoke when I had reached the end of the tale. "That's beautiful."

"It is?" I hadn't really heard it. My mind was with Ali. I wondered what was wrong with him. I wondered if it was my fault.

"You okay, little man?" asked Marlene.

"Yeah." I lied. "What did I do to make Ali sick?"

`She covered her eyes with her hands in exasperation. "You think that you did something? You think you are God, don't you? You think you are in control of everything. You think you are so far above the rest of us, that you cannot make any mistakes? You can't fail? You did miss the point of the story, didn't you?"

"What's going to happen to him?"

"Listen, Cole, I don't know what's wrong with him." Marlene shook her head. "We can't control what happens, Cole."

"No, you're right. I'm not in control, and that scares me."

Marlene's voice was gentle. "None of us are in control. I couldn't control my daughter. You can't control Ali's illness. Maybe our lives are like storybooks. Maybe the plot is written, and we just need the strength to turn the page and read."

An idea flashed into my head. "The plot. The story. Marlene, don't you see? The book and the tales are leading me. What happens in the Master's stories happen in my life." I snatched up the purple book. "I'll read ahead. I'll read the ending. Then I'll know."

I flipped the pages to the end of the book. The strange calligraphy, black on the white page, was there. The end of the book. The end of the story. All the answers on a single page. But my eyes couldn't focus on it. I flipped back madly through the tales. Words were there, but I couldn't seem to read them, not even a single letter. Like a dream where you know what you have to do, but you can't do it. My eyes wouldn't work. My brain couldn't make sense of the markings. I flipped back further. There were words, but no words, until I reached the "Forest Tale." Then, I could read again.

"What does it say?" asked Marlene.

"I can't read it."

"What do you mean?"

I handed her the book, and she stared at one page after another. For the first time, she was as confused as I was.

"Sweet Mary's dirty veil. Can't read ahead, can ya? Amazing."

Despair washed over me. "What's going to happen to Ali, Marlene?"

Marlene stared at the book and smiled. It's a wonder, Cole. Or is it magic? Odd. Ali? I don't know what's going to happen to him. I'm no fortune teller."

A light went off in my skull. I headed for the door.

Marlene shouted after me, "Hey! Where are you going?"

The screen door slammed behind me before her last word reached me. "I'm going to find out what's going to happen!"

I was already to the sidewalk. I'd passed Hope sitting in the middle of the driveway on the way. The little girl was a pool of opal in the sunlight. Sitting cross legged, her gaze was locked on Ali's front door. Hope was keeping vigil.

I headed away from uptown, the sound of Marlene trying to

pry the chair off her butt fading behind me. Donnie from the fertilizer plant was towing an anhydrous tank through town. I acknowledged the pointer finger salutation from his steering wheel and kept up the pace all the way to The Owl House.

The old place was an architectural oddity. Small by Antique Row standards, the house had been built in the 1880s and, like I said before, fit its name. It was painted, peach and orange and bright yellow with brown trim. Not to belabor the obvious, it looked like an owl dressed up for Mardi Gras.

Georgia Jasper stood on the side porch watering a flower planter full of freshly planted geraniums. When she saw me coming, she dropped the watering can and turned for the door, but she hadn't been alert enough, and I was on the porch grabbing the storm door before she could close it. There was a little twitch of panic on her face. Georgia always had that hyper-vigilant cat thing going. In this case, her wary senses had failed her.

"What do you want, Cole Seatstone?" She was tugging the metal door closed.

"I need to talk to you, Georgia." I was tugging it open. The door was at equilibrium.

"You didn't want to talk this morning." She was pissed. "I got to take care of the kids. I've got no time for you." She held on to the handle.

"Don't give me that. The girls are with their dad in Council Bluffs. The boys are with their dad in Des Moines. Everybody knows the visitation schedule, Georgia."

"I gotta get to work." She tugged, but I was braced now.

"Nancy works Saturdays. You don't work 'til tomorrow." In a small town there are few secrets. There are a lot of things people don't talk about, but there are few secrets. Georgia had been married six times. You'd be surprised how common that is out here in the hinterland. She'd hitched up with a rodeo cowboy, three long haul truckers, a farmer and her current mate was a hell of a woodcarver named Albert, not Al. Now, Albert and Georgia were divorced, too.

But they were still living together for some reason that she had explained to me one night at the bar. If I ever had understood the rationale, I had certainly forgotten it by the time the next pitcher of beer had arrived.

Albert was a helluva guy. I liked him. He was an old hippie like me. We had a lot in common. That was probably why he didn't like me much. You had to admire Georgia. All of her husbands were nice guys. The remarkable part was that she had packed all that romance into eleven years. She was only thirty-two and quite pretty, by any standard.

"I don't want to talk to you, Cole. I have a headache already." Her blond hair was up in a bun today, and she was wearing a classic country outfit, blue jeans and a work shirt. Her belt buckle was filigreed silver and her sneakers were brand new white.

"Georgia, it's very important."

"Don't be bringing me that book back," referring to her attempt to decapitate me earlier in the day. "I never want to see one of your books again."

"The book? One of my books?" I wasn't following her.

"It was one of your worst. I don't know why I was reading it again. I guess I hoped..." Georgia was getting that dreamy look.

"Do you mean the Doctor Finch book? The one with the old tales and...?"

"Stop acting like an ass, Cole. You know which book I'm talking about, that novel of yours about the small town and the lovers..." She was tearing up now.

"Wait. What book did you throw at me?"

Her voice was cracking. "The one you gave me. 'Lost in Old Wood' by Cole Seatstone." Was it sarcasm or pain in her voice? I couldn't tell. "The one you gave me. The one you wrote in. 'To Georgia, you see the future, a future I wish that I could see.' That book, you idiot."

My brain was churning, "But Ali got it out of the bushes, and it wasn't my book. It was..."

"You are something, Cole. Look over there. I can still see that damned book in the branches where it landed." She pointed out towards the big forsythia bush by the street. I could see the red book in the branches about six feet up. "There's your book, and your future. You can keep it all."

"But, Ali... Where did the purple book come from? What's going on?" The day had started so simply. I knew exactly what was going to happen. Now, everything seemed out of control.

"I know what's going on, Cole. Poor Cole. Poor little Cole. You're coming to me again for answers. And I..." Her voice drifted off.

"Georgia, I..."

"Another crisis, Cole? It's too late to save the marriage. I saw the truck this morning. I offered you help. Sophia finally left. Surprised it took her so long. Nothing I can do for you." She gave a hard pull on the door, but I was ready for her, and I snatched it back. Her hand slipped off the handle. Now I was blocking the open door. She was on the threshold unprotected.

"Georgia, please, I need to talk to you. It's about Ali." I used my smoothest voice.

She surrendered. "Okay, okay. C'mon in. But it'll have to be quick." She turned and headed into the kitchen. A black and white cat scooted in the opposite direction as I stepped in. The cat's ivory tipped tail snaked out as the door closed behind me.

"Damn, you let Nebedchadnezzar out!" Georgia had four or five cats all named for one Biblical figure or another. Moses got run over by a tractor last year. The rest, I can't keep their names straight, rarely even moved. One at least, a gray named Absolom, was always posed in one of the big owl eyes. Except for an occasional twitch of the tail, he might have been mummified. He was always there watching. That's what cats do best.

What Georgia did best was divine the future. Everybody in Sycamore thought of her as a fortune teller, except Honey, down at the restaurant. Albert, the woodcarver, had been Honey's husband. Honey thought of Georgia as a home wrecker. Georgia preferred to be called an intuitive. She had a website and did quite well. The Owl House was freshly painted, and the furniture was mostly leather.

Georgia led me into the Reading Room. It had been a parlor once. Now the dark wood room was where psychic connections could be made. The walls were lined with shelves holding statues and odd collectables. A bust of Aristotle was next to a Lando Calrisian figure. A Hummel shepherdess was flanked by a Roy Roger's lunch box and a pewter dragon holding a crystal. The effect was beyond eclectic. The scene was disorienting.

She sat on a mahogany high back chair. I paced back and forth.

"Now, what do you need to know, Cole? And please sit down!" Georgia was irritated. She remembered our past meetings differently than I. Maybe she was mad at me because I'd made a pass at her, or maybe she was down on me because I hadn't. I couldn't remember a thing.

I sat down on a green stuffed chair that was too low. The cushion was excessively soft and I sank down so that with my feet on the floor, my knees ended up even with my shoulders. Georgia didn't want me comfortable.

"Ali's sick. He passed out kinda. I need to know he'll be okay." I saw no need to beat around the bush.

"I don't work that way, Cole. You know that."

"You said there would be a death tonight."

"Sorry. I was angry, Cole."

"You said it like a curse." The words made her flinch, like I'd slapped her.

I knew how she worked. I'd seen her professionally just after Sophia and I moved here. At least I told myself it was all business - but I always send out confusing signals. Georgia's signals were obvious. I just chose to ignore them.

It was like visiting a beautiful dentist. Pleasure and pain. Curious to know if my novel would be an artistic success, she avoided that topic, and instead, out of the blue, she told me Sophia was unhappy. Would it be a be a best seller? She ignored the question, and without me asking, Georgia told me that Sophia was going to leave me. Did that make her a good intuitive? Let's just say everyone I asked said the same thing. That future was only invisible to one person in the world – me.

It was important to me that I know what was going to happen to Ali. Losing him was frightening now. One child was already gone. If I knew the future, maybe it could be changed. If I'd listened to Georgia when she told me about my wife, maybe that outcome would have been different. I would listen this time. This time I would not miss the future. This time I would change it.

"What will happen with Ali?"

"All right, no ceremony for you." Georgia's face closed. Almost like it went out of focus. Then, her features cleared again. Maybe my eyes were blurring.

"What about Ali?" I was in a hurry.

Georgia didn't string it out. I should have been grateful. I wasn't.

She closed her eyes and opened them. She looked straight at me. "Ali is going to die."

There was a silence. Everything went out of focus again.

"What did you say?" I wasn't hearing correctly. There was a ringing in my ears.

"Ali is going to die. My God, Ali is going to die."

"What?"

She had seemed shocked when she heard her own words. I think she had expected me to be the one who would die. She must have picked up on my suicidal intentions earlier. That's what I thought. No, that's what I hoped. I wanted to die. I didn't want anything to happen to Ali.

She repeated sadly, "Ali is going to die." She looked at me like it was my fault. I'd seen that look in another woman's eyes, when a different child had been in my care.

"Georgia, I..."

Her face recovered its anger. "You asked. You wanted to know. Now you do. Leave your money on the kitchen table. If the cat is by the door, let him back in. Goodbye, Cole." Georgia stood up and left the room. I heard her tread going upstairs. I heard a door close.

I sat in that chair, swallowed by it. I listened to six cars pass by outside. I counted nineteen red squares on the rug. There were five male statues on the southern wall and seven female figures, twenty-two cracks in the ceiling and two cat's eyes staring at me from the doorway. Was it Job?

I didn't remember leaving. I wandered home on instinct. Marlene opened the door for me.

My body fell against her, exhausted, and I wept into her breasts. She held me close, and she stroked my head. Hope remained in the driveway. Waiting.

Marlene eventually brought me a glass of wine from my fridge. It was red wine in a blue tumbler. I sipped on it. Marlene drank hers with gusto from a green plastic cup. Sophia hadn't left me any crystal. Marlene refilled her cup. Then, she opened the little purple book and read me another tale.

I needed to listen very closely.

XXVI
The Tale of the Fish and the Oyster

Faltering were my Master's steps from the peak near the Forest of a Thousand Thousand Years. And the day was the color of Widow's Tree bark.

On the seventh day of this wandering, we reached a wall of many stone blocks carved wondrously fine. And at the joining between each smooth gray block and the next, the hair of a babe could not be passed.

My Master's steps took him to that wall, and he stopped and placed his forehead upon its cold face. My Master's voice was thin.

"Brown one, we have come to the Limit of Time."

My heart was troubled by this. For the story of this wall was known to me and had troubled my dreams as a child.

This was not a place of the world, for it was beyond the world. Children would shudder at the mention of this place that was not a place.

It is written:

> *The Limit of Time was not built*
> *it was not raised by hands.*
> *Adamant as all the lands*
> *stone not stone it stands.*
> *There do we part and there do weep*
> *stone not stone it sunders.*
> *There is the parting place*
> *time not time it thunders.*

My voice pleaded with my Master, "Can we not go back? Go back the way we came? Can we not begin again? Can things not be the same?"

And my Master fell to the ground and said, "Brown one, this is not ending. Teach me with your steadfastness."

And I sat beside my Master and we waited by that wall.

As far as the eye could see to the East, the Limit of Time was unbroken.

As far as the eye could see to the West, the Limit of Time was unbroken.

But my eyes, still young, saw just then a shadow, as if a door had opened. And that door was at the end of the West. And my eyes did see a shadow move from that door, and that shadow moved towards my Master and I, though the door the shadow came from was at the end of West, and we were at the end of East. It came without hesitating. Though the journey that faced the shadow was almost forever, it came. Many days my Master and I sat in the waiting. Every day the fever on my Master's brow waxed and waned. The sun made each trip in noisome progress. The Smiling Moon became the Maiden's Moon, became the Mother's Moon, became the Hag's Moon, became the Frowning Moon. The shadow became a figure.

The figure was a statue of stone. The statue had no face but was smooth and unmarked, and the great stone legs made no sound as they moved without moving, and the statue was beside us. The great stone figure was thirty feet tall.

I had no words, for it had no ears.

But the figure had a voice, and the ground hummed with the voice.

"This is the Limit of Time. Time comes for this old one."

I had no words, for it had no ears.

The stone arms lifted my Master. The arms were neither kind nor cruel. The stone arms lifted my Master, and then the voice spoke to me. "If you would save this old one, send a fish here of its own will. Of the fish's own will must it come to the door."

I had no words, for it had no ears.

And the ground hummed again.

"If you would save yourself, cause an oyster to give this wall a pearl freely. The oyster shall give freely, or you will not be saved.

And the statue turned, and with my Master, disappeared into shadow in the West. They did enter the hidden door and the hidden door did close.

My path led to the sea. For a hundred days, I did walk, and I came to the Sea of Floating Seeds. My path took me into the sea and under the sea. I walked among reefs of color and broken ships of man. I walked among swimming shark and walking crab. I walked until a fish of gold swam before me.

I called the golden fish. "Fish, would you hear my words?"

The fish replied, "Your words are heard, though you should not be here, man walker, though you swim in this sea like a fish."

My voice was strong in the water. "Would you aid me, fish? Would you travel of your own will to the Limit of Time, and free my Master?"

The fish replied, "I am a fish. I have no will of my own that can travel there. I swim in the sea. I eat and I am eaten. That is the limit of my will." With that the fish swam away.

But quickly, I reached out and took the fish by the tail. Holding the tail, I did eat the fish. For that was the will of the Golden Fish.

Beneath the sea I walked. I walked among waving kelp and bubbling stones. I walked among jeweled eels and swimming vipers. I walked until a mighty oyster seven times my height loomed above me.

I called the titan oyster. "Oyster, would you hear my words?"

The oyster's voice was in the water. "Your words are heard, though you should not be here, man walker, though you swim in this sea like a fish."

My voice called out to it, "Would you aid me, oyster? Would you give your pearl freely to the door in the Limit of Time and save me?"

The oyster replied, "I can give nothing. My shell is made for closing. My meat is meant for holding. My pearls are meant for the sea."

And the titan oyster did suck in the waters. And the waters pulled me into him. There I was surrounded by a layer of pearl and could not move. The oyster spun time around me, and time by time, he covered me layer by layer until in the end, I was a pearl.

Then did the oyster spit me out into the sea. A mighty waterspout scoured the pearl that was my being from the bottom of that sea, and I was hurled into heaven on its winds. As I had risen, so did I fall as a pearl.

As a pearl, I rose through cloud and wind. As a pearl, I rose through the spheres into the secret night and beheld the wings of stars. As a pearl, I rose to Morning Greeter and Evening's Key.

In my falling I was bent by light. The falling was through the minds of birds and through the falcon's stoop, a plunge of fire in a sky of ice. I fell, unbreathing, and the earth loomed to smash me.

But I landed as on a cushion.

A woman caught me in her hand, and she was rich in flesh and fold. The woman's breasts were full and her belly swollen with a hundred children. The woman's thighs were as whole shocks of wheat.

The woman laughed when she caught the pearl. And placing the pearl in her teeth, she bit down and freed me, whereupon she laughed again.

The woman's name was Bumiya, which means earth. And she listened to my story, and she laughed again telling me, "Go now to the door in the Limit of Time, and aid the old one."

But I said, "I have no fish. I have no pearl. How can I aid him?"

And Bumiya said, "Ask."

So, I journeyed to the door of shadow in the wall of the Limit of Time and called out.

"Will you not give me my Master?"

The earth and the wall hummed its answer. "We know no Master here."

Puzzled, I remembered the manner of the statue.

"Will you give me the old one?"

There was silence, and the door opened without opening in the stone that was not stone. And in the wall that was not a wall, I thought I saw a fish swimming in its shadow. And in the door that was not a door, I thought I saw an indentation, and I thought I saw my hand place a pearl in that setting. The Limit of Time wavered and was gone from my eyes in that moment.

My Master came out, and he greeted me. "Well done, brown one. You have broken the Limit of Time. Are you a god after all?"

I kissed my Master's feet and said, "No, Master I am no god. I learned a lesson from the earth. Doors open when you ask."

My Master laughed.

"You learned to ask. And you swam in the sea until you became a fish. And you slept in the oyster until you became a pearl. And you came here to aid me of your own will freely. Think well, as will I, think well of what you have truly learned. Remember this well."

And so I have, and so I have told this to you.

XXVII
Asking

When the town whistle blows, I still twitch.

Its howl comes at seven in the morning, at noon, and finally at six in the early evening. We call it the town whistle, but of course, these days it's a siren. It also calls out when the volunteer firefighters or EMT folks are needed or when a tornado threatens. The sounding is an old custom for alerting farmers in the surrounding fields of the major time marks of every working day, Monday through Saturday.

That day, when the six o'clock whistle blew, I almost jumped out of my skin.

Marlene grabbed my arm to steady me. "You're shaking. Calm down now, little man. Calm down." She was still holding the little purple book.

The Limit of Time was still running through my head like a siren.

"I've got to get to Ali!" I headed toward the door, or I would have, but Marlene had leverage on me and a strong grip on the back of my belt. My feet moved, but my body didn't. I didn't have the torque to tow the fat woman more than six inches or so. I was in a cartoon.

"Hold on, little man. Hold on. You planning to just walk on into his house? It was my impression that Ali's mom is the private type. I didn't notice that she liked you much." Marlene was a font of wisdom. I would have slapped her but... I was afraid to. I wasn't afraid of her slapping me. My wife slapped me once. Sophia was just trying to get me to talk, to respond, to reappear. I wasn't afraid of Marlene slapping me, I was afraid of wanting to slap her.

Marlene spun me around with one meaty arm and roughly knocked me off balance. I ended up cross legged on the floor.

"Marlene, you trying to break my leg?" I thought she had

broken both of them.

"What can you do for Ali, anyway? Why do you care?" She produced the jar full of Ativan. She'd stowed the jar in her cleavage. "You were going to take these tonight, weren't you? What difference does Ali make in your sad little about-to-end world?"

"I don't want him to die." I was sinking back into my passive monotone.

"You think he's dying?"

"Georgia said he was."

Marlene sighed. "Georgia, the intuitive, told you, I know. Georgia, the fortune teller who predicted the end of your marriage, told you. Well excuse me, but I believe she predicted an earthquake last year."

I had to defend my source. "There was an earthquake, a big one in Chile, I think."

"You idiot, she predicted one for Iowa! Last time there was an earthquake here was when God dropped his bowling ball and killed all the dinosaurs." Marlene was smiling that white toothed smile again.

The absurdity of it saved me. "God's a bowler?"

"Yeah," said Marlene. "He likes those little shirts with the bowling pin buttons and his name on the pocket."

"That's silly. God doesn't need pockets."

"Sure he does. Gotta keep his Cuban cee-gars somewhere." Marlene laughed and so did I. "Besides, that fortune teller of yours also predicted the last six Super Bowls wrong, has never picked a Best Actor Oscar in her life, and once told me I was going to be a beauty queen."

I looked at Marlene. I liked what I saw. "You are beautiful, Marlene."

It surprised me when she reared back and slapped me. It wasn't a friendly slap either, it was a George Foreman Grill in a sock slap, and it knocked me flat.

Reality intruded, and Marlene shook herself out of that tight fitting chair like an obese female panther. She stood over me, pointing at me with a blood red fingernail on a pale sausage finger. "And you are married! What kind of a woman do you think I am? I'm a fat lonely girl? So I just swoon when a guy gives me the eye and a little sweet talk? Listen, Cole, I know I'm beautiful. I've been loved. And the man who loved me was twice the man you are! He was alive, and he was strong, and he held me, and his kisses were sweet!"

I thought she might step on me. "Marlene, I know..."

"Know?" She shouted. "You don't know anything. Life isn't something that happens in your intellect. This life you get isn't philosophy or art. Living is not happy hour. It's as real as mud. This is the real thing, Cole." Marlene was on a roll. I held very still.

"You think it's all over. You live in your head. And nothing quite measures up, does it? Everywhere you look you see ugly things. You see me as fat. You see shallow ignorant people. You see idiots and rubes. You see your own failures. If there's a beauty mark, you see a cancerous mole. Who do you think you are?!" Marlene turned away. "I need another glass of wine." She sounded disgusted, thoroughly disgusted.

I called after her. "I'm sorry, Marlene." She didn't respond.

A fly landed on my bare arm, another apology. I noticed the book next to my hand, on the floor.

The refrigerator clattered as Marlene looked for the bottle.

I opened *Tales of the Master* and I began to read.

At first my voice was timid, but it grew into the words of the story on the pages.

XXVIII
Tale of the Ugly Man

We journeyed, my Master and I, and there seemed no direction, no three steps without turning, for my Master's eyes were elsewhere than this world. And the day was freshly bled leather.

There before us, in that road, was a man.

And the man's body was covered with sores. Sores weeping with illness.

The man's legs were twisted and scarred. Scarred with hot iron wounds.

On his back were jagged pink ridges of tortured skin. Tortured by the whip.

His naked body was filthy with excrement. Filth from his own bowels.

Maggotts writhed upon his feet. Writhed at their supper.

His arms were covered with leeches and blisters. Blisters beyond healing.

Upon his face were burns and blackened skin. Skin unliving.

His lips cracked and covered in warts. Lips of no feeling.

The man's hair was matted with sweat and ditch mud. Sweat and mud.

But the man's voice was as a splash of wine into a cool clay cup.

And he said to us, "Greetings on this fine day. Soft be your steps on this hard road."

My Master saw the man with his eyes. The man was the first thing he beheld, that blood leather day. My Master had returned to the world. My Master began to whistle his song for the flying yellow birds once more.

And I approached the ugly man and embraced him. I embraced him in joy and love, and then I kissed the ugly man.

As we walked away from the ugly man, my Master smiled and whistled louder.

And my Master said to me, "What beauty. Take care to remember this."

And so I have, and so I have told this to you.

XXIX
Permission

Truth is where you find it.

One time I found my lost car keys in Sophia's panties. Don't laugh, it's true. There was a time when Sophia and I laughed all the time. The Ugly Man had made me think of my wife's beauty.

Marlene had listened to the tale from the kitchen. As short as it was, it had struck a chord with her, too. When she came back into the living room, she wasn't angry anymore.

"You're not going to hit me again, are you?" I had to be sure.

"No, you sweet little man, I'm not going to hit you again." She took a deep breath. "Unless you deserve it again." She smiled.

"How'd you get to be a door-to-door missionary?"

"I don't know. I started off selling Avon. I guess I got tired of taking people's money. I started asking them about God instead. Then, one day I knocked on a preacher's door and he got me all fired up." Marlene's eyes were drifting. I loved her eyes.

"All fired up?"

She smiled that knowing woman smile. "Well, that's where my daughter came from. I pray for her everyday."

Why she would pray so hard for a little girl like Hope was beyond me. I didn't want to go into the subject of prayer, so I asked instead, "This man of yours, is he dead?"

"No, that would have been easy. He had a stroke. He's in a nursing home up in Kanesville. He's still a lovely man. I visit him every Saturday. Lying in bed just kinda smiling, he's still a lovely man." Marlene dabbed at her eyes with a little flowered handkerchief that she tugged out of her cleavage. I wondered how much stuff was in there. "I just went on preaching like a madwoman. It was sort of in his honor. He was a good husband. He still supports me."

"He was rich?"

Marlene laughed. "Yes, he is rich, as rich as he needs to be. In his wild days he played poker. He won a couple hundred thousand at the big boat casino over by the Bluffs. He put every penny in the bank after he bought a house, so I have a place to live and a little food money. His insurance pays for the home, and I get a bit of an allowance from that, too. Ain't life funny?"

"What do you mean?" I asked.

"I was looking for God, and I found a husband. I was given a daughter. God help her. When he had his stroke, I thought I had to keep preaching. I started looking for people to save. I found you."

"And you're trying to save me?" I stepped away from her a little.

"I thought I was. Now, I'm not so sure. I don't have the power to save. Maybe I can help. That's different. I've learned that much."

"I still have to go to Ali."

She snorted. "So you can save him? That's a laugh."

When she put it that way, I knew it was absurd. "I know I can't save him, but he can help me. Maybe that's why I have to see him."

"Okay, little man. Let me see what I can do." Marlene started adjusting her bra straps again. That meant action. She went out the front door.

The evening was well underway now. In the spring, nights cool off quickly and there was a chill tang in the breeze as I followed her. Hope was still sitting like a yogi in the driveway, watching Ali's front door.

"Come here, honey." Marlene called her. Hope popped up and ran into her arms.

"Marlene, can I see Ali?" She had the sweetest voice.

"Let's find out, dear."

I started to follow them, but Marlene turned and gave me a look.

"What?" I said.

"Just let me handle this. You trot on down to the bar, and get me a bottle of wine. And take your time, I'll send word when we need you." There would be no argument. That was clear.

"Sure, Marlene. Thanks."

"Nicest thing you've said to me all day. Now run along." Marlene, with Hope in her arms, headed for Ali's. I headed uptown towards the bar. I was half a block up the street when I realized I still had the book in my hand. "What kind of wine goes with a purple book?" I wondered.

The bar was quiet. There were two farmers at the bar. Vern and Eldon were nice enough, and they never bothered me. Three people sat in one of the booths, I think they were from the county roads department. I didn't know them, they didn't know me. That was good, too.

I wasn't in the mood for socializing. I ordered a beer and tossed it down. Kenny, the bartender. watched me. Like any good bartender he knew his customers well. While I drank, he waited. When I set the empty mug down, he picked it up, refilled it, and only then, went back to his newspaper at the other end of the bar. I always drink the first one quickly.

That's when Hancock Jake walked in. He was a legend in town. He was a myth in three counties. He was a folk tale in the state of Iowa. Hancock Jake was a certified town drunk, but he had taken this avocation to new heights of artistry. Jake always ended his drinking sprees in spectacular fashion.

They had found him unconscious and naked in the arms of the "Unknown Presbyterian," a statue of some old preacher over in Bellow Wood. Jake had turned up passed out and naked on a table in Mishka's Pancake House when they opened one Easter Sunday morning. He was discovered snoring and naked on Beverly Jebber's La-Z-Boy when she came downstairs one Tuesday to see why her blind corgi was barking. Jake had thrown up on the poor dog.

Jake threw up often. He threw up on cars, on flower beds, on sheriff's deputies. Jake upchucked on sidewalks, tractors, Mrs. Lazar twice in one day, tombstones, and tourists. But Hancock Jake was most famous for his trademark behavior.

Jake would sit at the bar quietly drinking for five or six hours, and then he would push himself back slightly, use both hands to grasp and hold the top of his bib overalls away from his chest, tilt his head forward, and vomit into his Osh-Kosh. Then, he'd pat the bibs back into place, adjust his shoulder straps, and order another highball. I'd seen him do it on several occasions. The look of contentment on his face was always spiritual.

Nobody sat near Jake when he was drinking, but no one stopped him. He was considered an artist of sorts, though no one around Sycamore ever put it in those terms. Besides, after Jake threw up into his bibs, the betting started on where his naked, comatose body would be found the next day.

Jake came in the door, disgustingly sober, and plunked down next to me and my beer.

"Hey, Jake," I said, getting ready to move to another stool out of range.

"Hey, Cole." That was a whole lot of conversation for Jake, but his eyes widened as he spotted the little purple book I was holding. "What you got there?"

"Just a book, Jake." I protectively held it away from him.

"I've seen that book before." He pointed at the book. "I've seen that out to Doctor Finch's place."

I sat back down. "You knew Doctor Finch?" Jake wasn't likely to throw up for a couple hours yet, and the smell wasn't too bad with the breeze coming in the tavern's open door.

"Yep, I used to work for Doctor Finch and Master."

I almost threw up. "Master?"

"Yeah, can I get a drink?" Jake was losing interest in the conversation.

"Kenny! Kenny! Get over here and get old Jake a drink." I had to get ahold of myself and keep Jake on task, here.

Kenny didn't move from his stool at the end of the bar. "He still owes me twenty-five from last night. You still owe me twenty-five from last night, Jake."

I rummaged in my pocket and tossed fifty bucks or so on the bar. "I got that covered. Now give him a... What'll you have, Jake?"

"A Bushmills, straight up. A triple with a beer chaser." Jake didn't seem the least bit grateful. Neither did Kenny, but he took the money and delivered the poison.

"Did you say Doctor Finch and Master, Jake?"

He tossed down the Bushmills. "Yep, that's what I said. Great guys. I worked for 'em off and on for twenty-five or thirty years. Nice guys. Great guys. Good people." He was wiggling his empty glass at me.

"Another round here, Kenny!" Jake was not a cheap date. "Jake, was the Doctor's friend named Master?"

"Nah, his name was Tadessee or some kind of weird African name. I can't really pronounce it. There was some kinda click or noise in the middle like Ta-click-desse or something. But the Doc always called him Master. I called him Master, too, it was easier to pronounce." One gulp, and he wiggled his glass again.

"Kenny, leave the bottle." Jake was getting glassy eyed. "Jake, what were they like?"

"Well, they paid me well. Let me sleep in the house. Never yelled at me for drinking. They traveled all the time."

"Where'd they go?"

"All sorts of places. Africa, Turkey, India, they went everywhere. The Doc was rich. Rich women sent him money, I think. I saw a few come to visit. Saw some of the mail they sent, checks and such."

I was right. Finch was scamming money. "He was swindling them, wasn't he?"

Jake gulped down another two or three ounces of Bushmills. He grabbed his bibs. I started to back up as a look came over his face, but the moment passed.

"Swindling?" Jake thought for a second. "I don't think so. I saw the Doc give out more money than he brought in. Saw him refuse money from some of the ladies. I remember one day this biddy drove up in a big black car. She had a driver and everything, and she gets out and walks by me while I'm sweeping the porch, and she kinda sniffed at me like I was garbage and stuck her nose up in the air. Well, Doc saw her do that, I guess, and he kicked her out of the house. She was all fussy and cackling like an angry hen when she left. If he was swindling them, he was picky about it." Jake poured another triple.

"Why'd they go to Africa and Turkey and those places?"

"They was running hospitals and orphanages and schools and things like that. They got all sorts of pictures from all over the world sent to 'em of stuff like that. Doc helped some folks get out of trouble over there. He hooked that Moslem guy up with the Baptist preacher. Got him outta some trouble. Doc died right after the poor guy got over here, though."

Jake downed another drink, and his eyes clouded over.

Hospitals, schools, orphanages...it wasn't the answer I expected. Doctor Finch had gotten Ali's family into the States. That was a bit of coincidence that clanged when it hit my brain pan. "What was Master like? Did he run the show?"

"No, he was just a sweet man. Doc did everything for him, and I never heard Master ask or order or anything. Then when Doc died..." Jake drifted back to his glass.

"What happened when Doctor Finch died?" I could tell this was important.

Jake looked sad. He looked drunk, but he looked sad, too. "After Doc died, Master came to me and... hell," I think Jake was tearing up. "...Master came to me and said, 'Now you will be my Master, Jake.' That's what he said to me. He said I'd be his Master."

"What happened, then?"

"Master started doing everything for me. He said I was teaching him stuff just by being me. I'd go out and get drunk, and I'd wake up all clean, and he'd be sitting with me. But I didn't like being the master that way. Made me feel funny, so I left."

"Master said you were the Master?" I was confused. My ears were warm.

"Yeah. Crazy, huh? Me, the Master. But, you got the book

now, so you must be the Master now." He pointed at the purple book on the bar.

"Having the book makes me the Master?"

"When Tadessee told me I was Master, he gave me the book. I tried to read it but, well, I don't know. Like I said, I couldn't be no Master. Now, you got the book. You must be the Master."

"What does that mean?"

Jake didn't answer. He just grabbed his bibs, pulled 'em away from his chest and tilting his head forward, threw up.

I moved to an empty booth upwind and opened the book.

XXX
The Tale of the Prophet

In those days, we were lost. Though we did not know.

Beyond, we traveled where none had gone, for the Limit had been breached, and the sky was unclear in those days of walking. And then the day dawned red. And I was unsure in my steps.

My Master and I entered a cave. The cave was a hole in the fabric of that day. The cave was an unseen mirage. The cave was a silent sound and a vision of blindness. My heart had no pulse, and my blood had no warmth. The day lost its color, for it was darkness, and in that cave our eyes were blind.

For a time, we struggled on, past the stirring of black bats and white snakes, though neither could we see, but rather we felt them on the ends of our hair and in the air moving above us and the water rippling at our ankles. Unmoving wind and a chaos of stillness enveloped us. Into the cave we ventured, until my Master touched my arm, and we stopped.

We stood in the home of the Prophet.

The Prophet's face was unknowable in that blackness. The Prophet was a rumor of that age, and the Prophet's legend was a whispered warning in all the lands. It was said that the fates and futures were snakes and spiders. It was said that fruit unripened was as poison. It was said that only jackals knew where the doe would die. It was said that finding a key before it was lost melted seals and locks. It was said that gain was subtracted in a mirror of knowing. All these things were said.

We stood in the home of the Prophet.

My Master was beside me, but I was alone. My Master waited for my voice. I could not speak. There was a coldness in me. My sin was within me.

From silence layered like sandstone, came the Prophet's voice. From lines of razor sharp flint and the slickness of the shale that burns, came the voice. My ears could see. My eyes could hear.

The voice of the Prophet:
"The brown one stands in darkness before me. He has traveled far. He has reached this darkness. He has been boy and man. Son and stranger. Amazement and amazed. Friend and enemy. Husband and wifeless. Dung and fly. Forest and leaf. Water and treasure. Naked and exhausted. Fish, oyster, and healer. Swimmer, walker, pearl, and now nothing. The brown one stands before the Prophet. Ask, and I shall answer you now."

I was the brown one, and I was all the things the Prophet said. I stood in darkness, and my Master's presence was lost to me. I searched my mind and found a thousand questions. My body prickled with a thousand questions. My spirit swirled in a fog of a thousand questions. My soul was overflowing with a thousand questions. But in my being, I found only being. Then in my being, I found my voice. My voice was wordless, and my voice was the sound of the unsaid.

I stood before the Prophet, and I was still.

The voice of the Prophet:

"The brown one stands in silence before me. There are no questions. There is no seeking in the brown one as he stands here. All graves can be opened. All sweet streams can be tasted. All pain made pleasure and all time held in his small hand. Yet he does not ask. The traveler, the pilgrim, the mastered, and the Master stand here and ask nothing."

I stood before the Prophet, and I felt life in my veins. I felt warmth in my blood, and I asked no question. That is when the answer was given.

The voice of the Prophet:

"Without question, I cannot but answer with a vision. Behold, brown one. Behold the face of the one who holds all time, all life, and all answers. Behold the face of life and death."

And in that moment, I saw the Prophet's face. And then I saw my choice.

The face was brown, and the black hair curled in the wind of Mada.

The face was my own.

My Master spoke. "Truth is near to you now. Take care to remember this well."

And so I have, and so I have told this to you.

XXXI
Faces

In the mirror behind the bar my face looked thin.

When I finished reading the story, I stood up from the booth and went to the bar to look at my reflection. My face was thin. I hadn't been eating. Sophia had stopped cooking. Or had I stopped eating first? My memory was fragmented. Cause and effect were distorted. Every incident I recalled, started with my own pain. Sophia was a shadow. I couldn't even see her face clearly in my head. I closed my eyes, and I couldn't find her. When I looked at the mirror, all I saw was my own face, suspended above a big glass jar of pickled eggs. They floated, suspended in the brine, darkened by the vinegar and sunlight, Chinese hen's eggs under dirty crystal.

Next to my face on the smudged bar back was Hancock Jake's. I'd left my money on the bar and he'd spent it well. Jake was torched, and he'd done it in record time, thanks to me. I had an odd thought that he was so drunk that he shouldn't even leave a reflection, but there it was. He grabbed my shoulder as he lurched to his feet and pushed off me to stand wavering in the middle of the bar. Conversations stopped. I had never witnessed it before, but others had and knew what was about to happen.

Hancock Jake unbuckled the straps on his bibs, and they dropped like a rotted curtain at a derelict theater. His underwear had a lot of water damage and more. The sleeveless shirt ripped away in Jake's hands. His chest was covered in matted hair. It was like watching a Sasquatch movie. Everything was slow and blessedly indistinct. His shorts hit the floor, and I swear there was a thud. Jake kicked his legs, and then he reached down and tugged his right work boot off. Balancing and hopping on that bare foot, he proceeded to tug at his left boot and by some miracle, and no doubt his frequent practice at the task, he stayed upright until with a pop, it separated from his leg. Yes, Jake pulled off the boot and his left foot all at the same time.

He set the boot full of plastic left foot down on the bar with reverence and then, totally naked, he headed for the door. It was a scene from one of those cheap horror films you laugh at late at night. Naked Hancock Jake slapped his bare foot down and then thunked his left stub on the plank floor. Slap...thunk...slap...thunk...slap...thunk. A naked man walking side slope, Jake let the tavern door slam behind him.

Kenny the innkeeper brought the spectacle to its ritual close. "I got five bucks that says he'll be in the ditch south of town tomorrow morning."

Farmer Vern chirped in, "Maybe, Kenny. But usually he gets that left foot off quicker. I don't think he'll make the highway. I figure he'll be by the Pepsi machine by the blacksmith's shop."

Vern's pal, Eldon, had his own theory. "Nah, I think he's sweet on Jody Thompson again. Saw him wave at her yesterday. Used his whole hand. He'll end up on her porch swing."

All I could do was stare at Jake's foot, sitting there on the bar next to a half finished beer in a grimy glass. Encased in a muddy boot, an offering, a relic on a pagan altar, a magnificent sickly yellow plastic ankle sticking out of the leather.

I had to ask, "When did Jake lose his foot?"

"Oh, he loses it all the time. But somebody always finds it." Vern laughed.

"One time he left it on the back of a reefer trailer full of swinging beef that had stopped up at the Gas n' Grub. The trucker didn't find it until he got to Denver. He sent it back UPS." Eldon was almost giggling.

"God knows how many kids in minivans were haunted by the vision of that old disembodied foot westbound on I-80." Kenny snorted.

"But when did the foot get cut off?"

Vern settled down and answered me seriously. "Had to be fifteen years ago. It was one of Jake's first drunks. Well, one of his first naked drunks. He passed out in some road weeds. The county crew came by with the mower and didn't see him until they hit him. Cut the foot off clean. Doc Finch tried to reattach it, but the Doc was no surgeon."

"That's when Finch and his man took Jake in, wasn't it?" asked Eldon.

"Yeah, think so."

"Sure didn't help old Jake out much, though, did it?" said Kenny.

"Hey, he did have a few good years in there. But now..." Vern's voice trailed off.

The door slammed, and I turned to see Georgia Jasper standing there in all her blond glory.

"Cole Seatstone, I oughta kick your ass!" She seemed angry.

"Sit down, Georgia. Let me buy you a pickled egg." The old charm was still there.

Georgia looked good as she walked up to me. She knew how to walk. She was a real sight to see. Then, after she popped me right in the nose, my eyes watered up, and I really couldn't see her too well for a minute or two. She tossed me into a booth.

The men in the bar whooped and clapped.

Vern piped up, "Damn, Georgia. You didn't give us enough time to get our bets down on the fight!"

"Shut your ass up, Vern, or I'll give you one, and you can try to explain the black eye to your wife." That kind of quieted all the guys down. With her reputation, Georgia could destroy any man by rumor alone - small town girl power at its finest.

There was blood coming out of my nose. "There's blood coming out of my nose, Georgia."

"Don't be a whiner. I want to apologize."

I rubbed my nose and showed her the blood on my hand. "This was an apology?"

"Just shut up, will you? Just be quiet, and listen to me, Cole."

I was afraid she would hit me again. Or maybe I was afraid she wouldn't. "Okay, I'm listening."

"I'm sorry I said what I said about Ali." She had real pain on her face.

"Because he's not going to die, right? You only said he was going to die because you knew it would hurt me. That's it, right?" Ali wasn't going to die. I knew it. I didn't know it. I wanted to be rational. I didn't know what rational was.

Georgia shook her head. "No, Cole." She looked so sad.

"Why do you hate me, Georgia?"

"I don't hate you, Cole." She covered her face with her lovely hands. "That's why I hate you."

"That doesn't make sense."

Her hands came down slowly to reveal her eyes.

"Cole, you made me love you."

"Now, that's an old lyric."

Her eyes flashed. Her hand jerked. She almost hit me again. "Damn you, Cole! You moved to town, and you were so sweet. You listened to me. You didn't judge me. You didn't make a pass at me. You were so right. I thought you were so right."

She was wrong, of course. Sure, we'd had lunches. We'd talked. But I hadn't been sweet. I'd just been my normal invisible self. I didn't really listen to her. I just never interrupted her. I didn't withhold judgment. I just didn't care. I didn't make a pass like so many others had done, because I didn't have much energy for life. I was too lazy to sin. I was too demoralized to care about anything. I was invisible, so she could imagine me to be whatever she wanted. She'd paid attention to me, and I liked that. But there's never enough attention, never enough.

"I'm sorry, Georgia."

"I wanted your wife to leave you." She was intense now.

"You wanted her to leave me?"

"You are so stupid, so self-centered. You had no idea of my feelings, did you?"

"No." What else could I say?

"I wanted her to leave you. So, I said she would." She leaned across the table and lowered her voice. "I don't predict the future, Cole. I can't predict what's going to happen."

"I knew that." I didn't know anything.

"You don't understand. I don't predict the future, I control it."

"What?"

"When I say something will happen, it happens. Not because it was going to happen, but because I say it will happen."

She was totally crazy. I had to be very careful. I was always careful. I lived so carefully, sometimes you couldn't see me live at all.

"You have that much power?" I asked quietly.

"You don't believe me. You think I'm nuts." She was trembling.

"No, I don't think you're nuts, Georgia." I lied a little.

"And now I said Ali is going to die." She seemed ashamed.

"Yes."

"Maybe I am insane."

"Maybe you are. Maybe I am." I picked up *The Book of Stone* and rubbed the cover with my thumbs. The linen was soft.

"What's that?" Georgia reached over and touched the purple book. She touched it ever so lightly and pulled her hand away slowly.

"It's the book. The book Ali found in the forsythia bush after you threw it. I mean, after you threw the book at me."

"What? I threw that stupid novel of yours at... sorry." Georgia gave me another fair review. Everybody's a critic. "Sorry, it's not that bad..."

"No, that's okay," I lied again.

"I mean, Ali found that book? I don't understand."

"Neither do I, really. All I know is, you tossed one book, and Ali found another."

"What book is it?" She reached for the purple book, but I pulled it back out of her reach. I had become very protective of *The Tales* by then. Obsessed would be a good word.

"The book is called *Tales of the Master.*"

"Who's the Master?" she asked.

"That's hard to say. I mean, I think Ali is the Master. But Jake says whoever has the book is the Master."

"So you're the Master? Hancock Jake says you are the Master? Funny." Georgia seemed almost amused. I wasn't in the mood for amusement.

"Whatever, the book is full of really old stories, parables and stuff. And everything that happens in the book seems to be happening to me. I read a tale and the story seems to come alive in my own life."

"Like what?" Now the crazy lady was beginning to think that I was crazy. Funny how fast roles can switch.

"I read about black birds, and I see black birds. The tale talks about lost sons, and I find stray dogs. There's a story about magic, and Ali says "she" loves me. There's this thing about four wives and karma, and a fat missionary shows up with a little girl. I read about a woman by a fountain, and I remember my wife's name..." I was talking really fast, trying to get it all out.

"Slow down, Cole." Georgia looked concerned now.

"Wait, there's more. Did you know apologies are like flies? Really, a fly landed on me." I suddenly realized how right Georgia was. I was insane. "I gave up the thing that was making me happy because..." My voice trailed off as I realized the futility of explaining what the book seemed to be doing.

"That's crazy."

"Maybe it is. Maybe crazy isn't bad." I was trying to find a way to convince myself that this whole day wasn't a massive delusion. Hearing the facts out loud wasn't helping.

"So the book is foretelling the future?" Georgia seemed unconvinced.

I struck back. I do that well. "Don't tell me you don't believe in seeing the future, Georgia."

A little temper showed on her face, then faded. "Okay, you got me there, Cole. But you've got to admit, the whole thing sounds a bit odd, at the very least."

"Yes, it is. It's crazy, Georgia. But it's true."

Georgia sat back in the booth. "I need a drink."

That reminded me. Marlene wanted a bottle of wine. "Kenny, bring us a couple bottles of your finest refrigerated, screw top wine."

Kenny shouted back from the cooler. "Red, white or pink?"

I looked at Georgia.

"Pink," she said. She knew her screw top wine. I had to admire that.

"Pink it is, Kenny. Make it pink."

Georgia leaned forward and looked at the book carefully. "How does it work?"

I laughed.

"You making fun of me?" She could still hit me.

"No, I'm not." I settled back in the booth and opened the book.

"Let me read you a story, Georgia."

XXXII
The Tale of the Child

The Prophet's cave behind us, my face still before me in amazement, I walked beside my Master, and the ground grew soft beneath our feet. The path was made of leaf and flower, fallen and giving color to the way. The day was autumn's red.

We came to a slow flowing stream of brown water. The water was like tea, and the smell of it brewing was around us. On one side of that stream, we walked in the soft decay of leaf and flower. On the stream's far side, we saw only sand and rock, endless, towards red mountains and hidden paths. On one side of that stream, we walked.

When the sun was above us and our shadows were gone, my Master stopped in his steps and gazed long upon the stream.

He spoke to me. "Do you not see the child?"

I answered him. "Yes, Master, I have always seen the child."

For there was a child. And the child was a girl of brown hair and sharp eyes. And the child was beautiful and floating above the stream. As my Master and I had traveled along the stream, the child had glided in the air without wings or wind. The floating child had followed beside us as we walked the path of leaf and flower along the brown tea stream. "I have always seen the child."

My Master spoke again in some reproach. "But you have not told me of the child."

I answered, "Forgive me, Master."

My Master spoke to me then as he had always spoken to me, and the reproach was gone from his voice. His voice was sad. "If you had told me of the child, we could have crossed the stream and been closer to the end of this journey."

My voice was dry, and I said, "I do not seek the end, Master."

He replied, "No, you seek forever. But you know it is not to be. The child has long been in your eye. For you know, brown one, that the child is the bridge."

My Master was true. I told him, "What shall I do, Master?"

My Master said simply, "Teach me."

In my confusion, I awoke from the spell of my own face, my own face as the prophet. My own desires, my own fears, shaping my future, trapping me in my own web. For that spell had been upon me every step from the Prophet's cave. That spell had been upon me always.

"How can I teach you, Master?"

My Master laughed and said to me, "Teach me as you have always taught me. Lead me as you have always led me."

I said to him in obedience, "I will lead you. But tell me how to lead you, Master. For the child is a child to my eyes and not a bridge."

And my Master spoke clearly then, so that I could not misunderstand. "Cross the bridge. A bridge is never a bridge until you step upon its planks and feel it holding you above the stream. Cross the bridge."

I would obey my Master. And in that moment of my thought, I stretched out my thought like a foot over an abyss. The floating child became a bridge of oak that lived beneath our feet, and we crossed over.

All in that one moment of my decision. We crossed over into the sand and rocks and hidden paths. And the bridge grew branches and branches behind us. The green of the new tree drank the tea of the stream, and it grew tall. The tree grew so tall that we walked for six days before its crown was hidden by the horizon.

My Master said to me in that time, "Remember the child. Take care to remember this well."

And so I have, and so I have told this to you.

XXXIII
My Body

My nose had stopped bleeding, but it was starting to throb.

Georgia had a mean right hook. But all that seemed behind us now as I finished the story and closed the little book. My intuitive friend had settled down and was sipping at her cheap pink wine, sloshing the sweetness around her teeth and the words of the story around in her head.

The smell of the black plastic booth, Georgia's sweet musk perfume, and the vaguely chemical bouquet of the unfortunately tinted faux Merlot overcame the copper blood in my nose, and I smelled a memory. I remembered a poem my mother would recite to me when I was a child.

She'd be sipping on her own glass and rubbing my back, always a little too roughly. I must have been between two and three, and my mother would almost sing it to me:

> *Go to sleep, little baby, go to sleep now*
> *Rock a bye*
> *Not a peep, little baby, not a peep now*
> *Rock a bye*
> *Momma's night, little baby, momma's night now*
> *Shut your eyes*
> *Don't you fight, little baby, don't you fight now*
> *Shut your eyes*
> *If you should die before you wake*
> *I pray the Lord your soul to take*
> *Don't you wake, little baby, don't you wake now*

Bye oh Bye
For my sake, little baby, for my sake now
Bye oh Bye
Moon's above, little baby, moon's above now
Don't you die
I'm in love, little baby, I'm in love now
Don't you die
If you should wake before he goes
I pray the Lord will eat your toes

It was a curiously weird nursery rhyme. I suspect it was of her own composition. My mother was talented in her own way. No one ever did figure out what made her that way. At least no one ever told me. I grew up mostly with my aunt and uncle in Kansas City. Uncle John worked hard at a dirty job, and Aunt Belinda didn't spank me more than I deserved. I still respect what they did for me after Mom did what she did. I suspect it was a genetic problem. I really didn't want to know.

Georgia snapped me out of the nursery nightmare I was looping into. "You and Sophia never had any kids, did you?"

"No." I lied. She was an intuitive. She should be able to figure this out. I didn't feel like helping.

"Did you ever want any?" Georgia may have been a bad wife, but she seemed to be a great mom. Her kids were bright and sassy in a healthy way. You could tell she was a good mom.

"No. I mean... Yes, we did want to have a kid." I decided to tell part of the truth. I took a gulp of the wine straight from the bottle. The wine was too cold. I couldn't talk for a second.

"You did? Why didn't you have one then? Something wrong with you?" Georgia smiled. She loved it when things got personal.

"No, sorry to disappoint you. I'm a fertile little boy."

"Sophia?"

"No, nothing wrong with her. Don't ever think there was anything wrong with Sophia." I got a bit heavy on the emphasis there.

Georgia backed off. "Sorry, sorry. Why no kids then?"

I crossed the bridge. "We had a kid."

That shut her up for a moment as she pondered the implications. Georgia didn't have the social inhibitions to stop her from going on. Maybe that was a good thing, maybe not.

Georgia's voice was full of preemptive sympathy. "Did your baby die?"

I hated hearing that. "I pray the Lord her soul to take."

"Oh, my God. I'm so sorry, Cole. I'm so sorry." I think she was. There were even tears in her eyes.

The bridge didn't seem too solid beneath my feet, but I hurried on over. "We had a baby. I was always afraid of the idea. But Sophia and I went to Costa Rica to visit her grandmother in this little Pacific coast town. Brazalito was beautiful, very poor, but beautiful. I would sit in one of the dirt floor Sodas, restaurants kind of, and I would watch the kids go to school in the morning. I decided one day that Sophia and I should have a baby. She was so happy. We made that baby right on a seashell beach. Nine months later we had Fiona. She had Sophia's olive skin and her gorgeous brown hair. Only her eyes were mine. God, I loved her."

Georgia leaned forward. "What happened, Cole? I know it's none of my..."

"I was writing one day. Sophia was at the store, and I heard Fiona crying. I was in the middle of a sentence. I decided to let her wait. Then she was quiet again, and I finished a couple more pages. Sophia came home, put away some groceries. She went upstairs. I heard my wife scream." I hadn't told anyone about that day. I felt so sure of the verdict. I looked at Georgia and pronounced it. "I didn't go to Fiona when she cried..."

"God, Cole."

I took another hit of wine. My stomach didn't respond well. For a second I thought I might have to imitate Jake. Maybe I'd even rip my left foot off, too. I looked over at that big old lonely work boot on the bar. My heart almost stopped when I saw little Hope. Brown hair and skin, she was sitting on a barstool, her legs dangling and swinging. Her bright eyes locked on to Jake's foot.

"Hope, what are you doing here?"

The kid floated down off that stool and came to me. She held out her hand. "Marlene wants you."

Kids nowadays called their parents by their first names. I wouldn't have let my daughter do that.

"She wants you." Hope was insistent. I loved the voice and the words. "She wants you."

Hope and I headed out the door, hand in hand. Georgia followed and kept quiet. That was another little miracle. My legs were sore from all the walking around I'd done and from being stuffed into that tiny booth at the bar. My head hurt, and my stomach was still gurgling with the wine.

I looked back, and Georgia had the wine in her hand. There's no open container law I know of in Sycamore. The sun was just down, and the air was clean. Hope's little legs churned away, and we made it up the block to my house in a minute or less. Marlene was standing there in the drive with her hands on her hips. She wasn't smiling.

"How's Ali? Can I see Ali?" I had a bad feeling.

"Cool down. His mom'll let you see him, but not until his dad gets home. She doesn't want you in the house without her husband present." Marlene sounded like a lawyer.

"Why? I'm not going to..."

Marlene laid down the law. "That's the way it's going to be, Cole, so cool off." Marlene peeked around behind Hope and me. "And who's this carrying my wine, Cole? Do I have to' share the wine and you, sweet thing?" It was another side of this big woman I had never seen. There's a joke there. You make it.

"This is Georgia Jasper. Georgia, this is Marlene." I was perfectly polite. I get nervous when I'm around more than one woman. Hope, holding my hand, helped.

"Oh, we already know each other, little man. Georgia, sweetie, you still a fortune teller?" Marlene seemed friendly enough.

"Intuitive." Georgia didn't take it that way. Things could get tense. "You still a missionary, Marlene? Find any converts today?"

Thank God Marlene took it as a joke. That deep laugh of hers seemed to calm the water.

"Bring the wine inside, Georgia. Let's have a drink or two. And maybe another story from old Cole's book.

We had the drinks first.

XXXIV
The Tale of the Executioner

Away from the stream, into sand and rocks we walked. Up the mountain at the edge we walked, and then our feet did burn. A walk down a mountain is the hardest of walks, for one is tempted to hurry down. So my Master and I measured our pace and believed each step was precious. And the day was the red of a horse's blood. My Master sang a song for me that day.

> *Oh, god went walking on the road*
> *and pilgrims came behind.*
> *Oh, god was singing as he strode*
> *and no one knew his mind.*

> *His feet crushed those he knew had sinned*
> *cruel judgment in his eyes.*
> *His waving hands made deadly wind*
> *behind him came the flies.*

> *Oh, god went walking on the road*
> *he had no taste for wine*
> *Oh, traveler lighten well your load*
> *and drink a cup of mine.*

The Maiden's Breast Moon had become the Mother's Moon, full of milk, and the night was full of light. And the day of my Master's song followed.

Our road was among the cliffs of the eastern valley when the sound of a man came to our ears. The man's cries were from a ledge below the road and the man called out to us.

"Oh, travelers, will you aid me? I have tumbled off the road in my drunkenness, and now I have no way back to the road I must use. Here have I sat in my pain, waiting for six days, and none have come to my aid. Oh, travelers, will you aid me?"

And my Master answered him, "Has no one else passed this way?"

And the man replied in his pain, "Yes, traveler, many have passed. A priest did refuse me. A merchant and a shepherd did refuse me, and likewise did a miner and a poet refuse me. Many have passed, yet here I remain, and my throat grows ever drier, and my spirit nears despair."

Asked my Master, "Why did those others refuse you?"

And the fallen man answered, "I am an executioner and despised by the people. I am the executioner of this land, and I am feared and loathed. No man breaks bread with me. No man shares my cup. No man or beast will aid me now. Will you aid me? You are from a further land and have no fear in voice or eye. Will you aid me?"

And my Master spoke in command. "Tell me, fallen man. Tell me, executioner. Where does your path lead upon this road?"

The executioner spoke as from a grave below that road. "I am sent by the Governor of the Divine Garden to the village of The Calf to execute a man for his crimes."

My Master asked of the fallen man, "What were the crimes of this doomed man?"

And the fallen man answered, "He is condemned for his laughter. This man did laugh during the Month of Tears. It is our law that none do so, for this is a holy time of sadness and repentance. This man defied our law, and I am commanded to fulfill the law."

My Master demanded truth. "And who is this man who laughed?"

The man replied in truth. "His name is Small. He is a man of no wealth or power, though I am told he is beloved. Yet my employer demands my service, and his death is the price that must be paid."

My Master asked yet another question. "So, on your errand you slipped from the road in drunkenness. Why did you drink so deeply?".

The executioner replied, "I drink wine to forget."

And my Master replied in a sigh, "And I drink to remember."

Then my Master did turn to me and bid me let down my fiber rope to the fallen man. My Master would not be refused, and I did not seek to refuse him. I let down my rope, and the fallen man climbed up to the road.

And when he reached the road, he offered my Master his jug of wine but was refused. My Master refused the drink but bade the man to drink deeply. And so the man took a mighty draught of wine, and another for my Master's health he drank, and another in thanks for his rescue.

The executioner had a mighty sword upon his back, and it was black polished and razor sharp. The sword was of great weight and beheaded like an idle whisper. The executioner bowed to us and set out again on his appointed journey, and his steps led away to the village of The Calf. He was lost to our eyes as the road turned in the distance.

And my Master sat in the middle of the road and wept. He wept in the dust on that day, brown as the eye of a goat. And his tears were brown with the dust of the road. There were no words, only weeping, and I coiled my rope as my Master wept.

When the mother's milk of moonlight covered us, I dared to ask my Master why he wept, and he spoke then as a man fallen to a lonely ledge.

"It is a sad day, brown one, and so I cry."

I asked my Master, "Is the day sad because we have loosed the executioner?"

My Master's words were as a pebble in a stagnant pool. "I was born in the village of The Calf. I suckled and grew there, and my brother played with me in the field near the mill. And we threw stones and flew with birds. We swam as fish and climbed like the black squirrels in the oaks of our youth. And my brother's name is Small."

And so I learned the reach of my Master's kindness was without limit. For he had rescued the man sent to kill his laughing brother.

My Master waved his hand and stopped my thought.

"Do not admire me, brown one. We saved the executioner, because no man can be left to die when aid can be given. We saved the executioner, but we left him his wine. And in my heart, I do hope he will drink too deeply and fall again before he reaches the village of the calf. Forgive me my wish. I will not wish that he fall again. I wish him no harm. I only wish him much wine. I only wish him much forgetfulness. Forgive me my wish."

And I understood.

*My Master spoke again, "My brother's name is Small.
Take care to remember this."*

And so I have, and so I have told this to you.

XXXV
On a Ledge

How long can a day be?

The day my life changed seemed to be ruled by a different clock than the one I had become so comfortable with. That town whistle would blow, and I would leave my little prison on Main Street. I would leave quietly and leave Sophia bundled, sleeping or not sleeping, under her twenty pounds or so of blankets, leave her under that cotton weight that so comforted her. I would have my quiet breakfast. I would wander through the morning and the afternoon. I would return home and barely taste the food Sophia put on the table. Darkness would come, and I'd stare at my computer screen trying to see the poem under the glow. I'd wake up on the couch, and time would roll into another day as Sophia slept or didn't sleep beneath too many old quilts.

Time just ticked on, and I knew the ending.

But that day, time was different. I felt it. Quicker and slower, heavier and lighter, brighter and darker, that day was ruled by a different clock.

I looked at the display on my microwave. The LED flashed "12:00...12:00...12:00..."

Marlene snapped me out of my timeless trance, "Cole, why don't you screw the lid off that second bottle of wine? Georgia and I are getting thirsty."

"Sure." I looked at the pinkish wine in the bottle between my legs. The color clashed with the soft worn purple of the little book's cover. "Sure." I picked up the bottle and twisted the gold cap. My palms were sweaty. I couldn't grip it. I tried again and then just gave up. I didn't seem to have any strength at all in my hand.

Marlene grabbed it with one of her meaty hands. "I'll do it, little man." A quick clicking twist, and the sweet bouquet of a California factory popped out.

"Hold off on the wine, kids," Georgia called from the door. She was illuminated by headlights that played across her blond hair and glinted off her filigreed silver belt buckle. The light caught her, passed across her and moved on until she was silhouetted by the street globe at the curb outside.

"Is he home?' Marlene asked.

"He's home. Just pulled in. He's in the garage. Go talk to him, Cole."

"Yeah, you want to talk to little Ali, you got to talk to Big Ali." Marlene was tugging me to my feet.

"Okay. Let go, I'm getting up." I really didn't need encouragement. But I secretly appreciated Marlene's help standing up. I was unsteady and a bit dizzy.

I headed out the front door. On the way by Georgia, she whispered to me. "I'm sorry I said what I said, Cole."

"Yeah." I didn't even look at her.

I looked at my feet as I stepped outside, off the little concrete porch and onto my driveway. The neighboring drive was next to mine, separated by a narrow line of scraggly grass and weedy vetch. I watched my shoes cross that line. I turned down the gravelly strip that led between the houses and down a slight incline to the back of the lot and the detached old leaning garage next door. I looked up to see the overhead door had been closed, but there was a light on inside. Big Ali was in there. I could hear his cursing.

He was not a happy man. Everyone in town knew it, and they kept their distance. Some said people stayed away from him because he was different, you know, browner. Can't argue with the fact that there are racists everywhere. Can't argue with the fact that small towns can be, let's say, cliquish. Can't argue with the fact that Big Ali was just plain unpleasant, either. For whatever reason, I didn't really know the man other than an occasional surly nod as he backed by me, heading off to work at the processing plant over in Planters.

I'd heard all the stories about him. They didn't bother me. The frequent yelling he did at night came through my door and my windows and even, in the winter, through my walls. That bothered me. He ran his house with fear. I felt it. I wanted to see his son, my Master. That made me afraid, too, but I knocked on the side door of the garage.

"Who is it?" he snarled, from behind the flaking paint and soggy cardboard patched window pane of the door.

I had to clear my throat. There was a catch in my voice, but it wavered out. "It's Cole. Your neighbor, Cole. Can I come in?"

There was a pause. Then a lock clicked and the door cracked open. It didn't swing open in welcome. It was just a crack of light. Then another pause, and finally, "Come in then!"

I pushed the door and let it swing. Inside I could see the dusty red side of Big Ali's pickup. The garage was narrow and when I stepped in, I saw him around in front of the truck. Shadows were stark in the light of a single bare bulb hanging high in the peak of the roof's interior.

"What do you want?" Ali senior was short, stocky, dark featured to match his personality. His hair was dark and cut short on his head, military style. His eyes were sickly brown, surrounded by a yellow that spoke ominously about his liver. He had a belly hanging over his work pants. He was wearing his work coat, white stained with blood. On his belt was a knife with a long practical wood handle and a sheath that hinted of a long narrow practical blade.

"I wanted to talk to you about your son."

"Oh, you want to talk to me about my son?" He was mocking me. "You want money? Because you buy him food? You want money?"

"No."

"You want to talk to me about my son? You have no son, do you?" He reached onto the workbench and picked up a long neck bottle of beer. He took a long swig.

I may have sounded angry at that. "No."

"So relax, Mister Seatstone. Relax. Do you want a beer?"

There was no real hospitality in his voice, but I'd seen enough Westerns to know that when the bad guy offers you a drink, you take it.

"Sure, I'll have a beer."

Big Ali turned to an old refrigerator to the right of the workbench. When he opened the white door, the yellow light from inside gave his face a menacing pallor. The effect was momentary as the fridge's door clunked shut. He tossed me a longneck, and I caught it without thinking. As I twisted the cap off, I realized that dropping the bottle would have been the end of the conversation.

He took another long pull on his beer and watched me over the bottle. He was waiting for something. I took a gulp from my bottle, cold in my sweaty hand. That's what he wanted. He took up the subject he had left behind. "You have no son."

"No."

His black eyebrows went up, "Aha! Yes, you have no wife, either. You have no wife. I see the truck today. I see what happened."

"No, I have no wife. Sophia moved out today."

"Too bad for you, Mister Seatstone. Your wife was a pretty woman. She was not happy with you, eh?" He was stating the obvious.

"No, she was not happy." I wasn't going to explain my marriage to him. Hell, I couldn't even explain it to myself.

He didn't even listen to me but turned back to the old cooler and grabbed himself another bottle. His face glowed momentarily yellow again. "She was a very pretty woman. I could have made her happy." He tossed down at least half the beer. "I liked to see her. She was very pretty." He didn't mean pretty. I knew what he meant and what he meant to do. He wanted me to be angry.

I changed the subject. "I didn't know Baptists drank beer."

He laughed. There wasn't much mirth in it, but he laughed. "No. Baptists do not drink beer, or whiskey, or wine. They do not drink." It was a cruel, deep laugh. "Baptists do not drink. But I am not Baptist!" The anger was back.

"But, I thought the Baptists brought your family here? I see you take the family to church Sundays and Wednesday night."

"My family, yes, my family." He gave a weak laugh. "Oh, yes. I go to church. I go to the Baptist church." He finished his beer and grabbed another, flipped off the cap and took another pull. "But I am not Baptist. I must go there so that I can stay here in this land of freedom." The word "freedom" sounded like a curse in his mouth.

"I see."

"You do not see. I am Islam. I am Moslem, as you say here."

"I didn't think Moslems drank, either."

The laugh was really loud this time. He laughed with the bottle in his mouth. Then he lowered the bottle. "Moslems do not drink. But I do." He was very drunk. He'd been drinking before he came home. "I drink because here is freedom!" He raised the bottle in a toast, and I raised mine in response.

"Freedom."

"Freedom! I will tell you something, Mister Seatstone. I will tell you because no one likes you in this town. No one likes you, and no one likes me. So I will tell you a secret. I am not a Kurd."

"You're not?" I just wanted to talk to little Ali.

"I was a Kurd. But I am now an American." He laughed and toasted a small American flag on the antenna of his truck. "I am an American!" There was more than danger in the air. All of a sudden there was something evil in the garage. Big Ali's face had changed. He took another drink and approached me. "I am once Kurd. But Iraqi government come to me. Sadaam men come to me. We call them moustache men. They tell me they will kill my wife - my beautiful wife. My wife! You have no wife, but you understand?"

I sipped more beer. My throat was very dry. "Yes, I understand."

"So I work for them. I inform on Kurds. They killed Kurds. It was my job to protect my wife. They kept their promise. The moustache men did not kill her." Big Ali drained his bottle and wiped his mouth so hard he might have been trying to erase it. "Sadaam's brave men did not kill her. They raped her. They made her barren!"

"I understand."

I had never seen so much pain on a stranger's face.

Big Ali straightened. "They said they would kill her unless I betrayed the Kurd leader. I told them what they wanted to hear. I told them about the Kurd leader. The men left my house. They left me to comfort my wife. The moustache men went to the Kurd leader's house and killed him. They killed his wife." Big Ali sobbed and struggled to find air in his lungs.

"Terrible. Terrible." I didn't know what else to say.

"You do not know. I ran to stop them when I realized what I had done in my selfishness. The leader was my brother. My brother! Do you see now?" He was shouting again.

"I don't know what..."

He cut off my pathetic words. "You do not know! I betrayed my brother! I ran to stop them, but I was too late. He was dead. With a piece of wire around his neck, he was dead and his wife was dead. Only their child lived. Only my brother's son lived. He was just a babe. And the people of the village saw it happen and saw me talking to the men, and they knew." The words poured out of him.

He took a shuddering breath and went on, quieter now. "Then I discovered that someone was going to kill me. The Kurds were going to kill me because they found out I was Sadaam's. The Sunnis were going to kill me because they kill Kurds. The Turks? They kill everybody. They came to kill me. Everybody would kill me. I became a Baptist, and I came here to this land."

"Doctor Finch and Tadesse saved you?"

"Yes, they saved me." He did not sound grateful. "They came and took me and my wife away and hid us in a hospital they ran, across the Turkish border. They gave me my brother's child to care for. They told me to be the child's Master." Big Ali shook his head sadly. "Be his Master... And now I live in freedom!" He made another mocking toast and a bow to the flag.

I backed up, "So you..." I had no idea what to say.

"Doctor Finch wanted me to be the boy's Master."

"He wanted you...?"

Big Ali cut me off with a killing look. "To be a master. To

live with no God. I could not be a master. I am a killer. I am an executioner. Do you not see that on my face?"

I saw the killing on his face, but there was something else too. I'd seen the same thing on my face in the barroom mirror. He had a trapped look.

"I cannot be master. God is the Master, yes? I would rather be Baptist. Baptists are sure of things. I need to be sure of things." He was running out of anger. His shoulders were slumping.

"Did Doctor Finch show you the book?"

He smiled and took a long drink. "Ah, the book. The purple book. The pagan book from Mada. We Kurds know of this book. It is of the ancient infidels. There is no God in that book. I would rather be a Baptist."

"But..."

"So you want to talk to my son?" He was fingering the knife on his belt. The book was a closed subject.

I couldn't stop looking at the knife. "Yes, I want..."

"You like my knife?" He had it out in one smooth move. A beer in one hand, a knife in the other, he moved towards me. "You know what I kill with this knife?" He waved it under my chin.

I tried to answer, but I had no answer.

He laughed. There was madness in it now. "I kill pigs!" He laughed again louder, then shouted. "I kill pigs! I am a Moslem, and I come to this land as a Baptist, and I drink..." He finished the beer and smashed the bottle on the concrete floor. The glass shattered and skittered everywhere. "...and I kill pigs all day. Unclean pigs!" He whipped around and headed back to the old refrigerator.

I finally took a breath. I searched for a way to defuse him. "You...you just do a job. You make a living for your family."

He stood at the open fridge, his back to me. "Yes, I make a living." He was quiet now. "Leave me alone now. If you want to talk to the son who is not my son, go. Talk to him."

I edged towards the door. "Thank you."

"Yes, thank me." Still turned away from me he had opened

another bottle. "You should talk to him. He likes you." At that he turned, and though his tone remained subdued, his eyes flashed. "He likes you. And he will be dead soon. It is sad."

I was dizzy again. "He'll be dead?"

"Ali has a bad heart." He pointed at his own chest, "Ali needs a new heart." His finger tapped on his own chest. "I do not understand it. The Baptist man says we will pray. Hah!" He took yet another drink. "We will pray! We will pray, and it will be another death on me."

"But..."

"Go! Go see him. I do not care." He turned his back.

I left the garage. I closed the rickety door until I heard the lock click. I walked back up the drive. I dropped the longneck in the grass and raised my arm in the dim light.

The watch on my wrist had stopped running.

XXXVI
The Tale of Three

The road reached the sea. All roads must reach the sea, and this road reached the sea in sorrow. At the end of this road were three poor villages. The houses were huts and the bins were holes, yet the people were proud beyond measure. And the day was purple.

The name of the first village was War, and the god of the village was depicted in a thousand statues. The statues stood everywhere. Strong legs and muscled arms. Golden swords in massive hands. Chests clad in armour. Thick, stubborn necks. And above the necks, smooth stone and an unfinished head. The people therein were armored and armed, and their children played as warriors.

My Master and I entered the village of War and walked among the people.

And the people said to us, "Have you seen our god?"

My Master answered them saying, "Yes, we have seen him."

And the people said to us, "What does he look like?"

*My Master raised up his right arm and answered them,
"He looks like a traveler."*

And the shout went up from the people.

"Be gone! Our god could never look like you."

My Master raised his left arm and shouted as they had shouted,
"Then your god will remain without a face."

And we passed through that village.

And the second village was named Pure, and the god of the village was
jealous. The god of the village demanded worship. The people therein were
clothed in prayer shawls and ashes, and their children played in silence.

My Master and I entered the village of Pure and walked among the people.

And the people said to us, "Are you men of prayer?"

And my Master answered them, "Yes, we are men of prayer."

And the people entreated us, "Do you bring us the prayer our god
wishes to hear?"

My Master raised up his right arm and answered them, "Yes, we bring his
prayer. You must pray that he does not notice you."

And a shout went up from the people. "Be gone! Our god must know us, or
we will perish."

My Master raised up his left arm and shouted as they had shouted, "Then
let your god notice you. You will perish still."

And we passed through that village.

And the third village was named Secret, and the god of the village was
unknowable. The god of the village demanded ignorance. The people therein
wore scarves of wool to muffle their voices and wandered without meaning,
and their children did not know how to play.

My Master and I entered the village of Secret and walked among the people.

And the people did not know us but spoke to our ears while looking away from us. "Are you men of knowledge?"

And my Master answered them, "No, we are men of many miles."

And the people asked, "Then you do not know the unknowable?"

My Master answered them, "We do not know what we cannot know."

The people of the village grew terrible and angry. "If you know that you cannot know, you know too much, and so you must die!"

My Master urged me to flee, and our running steps brought us to a boat. And taking the tiller, my Master bade me cast off the line and raise sail, so that we reached the waters where the people could not lay hand or club upon us.

And onto the sea we did venture. Behind us, the village of Secret was consumed by flames, as word of our knowledge burned through that place. And flames of worship and war burned in that village.

At the tiller, my Master found his breath, and said to me, "Truly, brown one, we have seen god's face and we have heard god's prayer. And also to our great danger, truly, we know too many gods. Gods are dangerous and silly by their very nature."

My Master laughed, and so did I. Through his mirth he said to me, "Take care what you know, and take care to remember this."

And so I have, and so I have told this to you.

XXXVII
A Reunion

There was a bruise on my hand, and I didn't know how it got there.

After I left the garage, I went straight to Ali. I noticed the bruise as I closed the little book. Ali had wanted a story as soon as I sat down in the small wooden chair by his bed. The room was small, little more than a closet. But the walls were covered in pictures that spread the world out before his eyes on the cracked plaster walls. The Parthenon, the Pyramids, the Empire State Building, and an empty stretch of white sand beach on a coral cove surrounded him.

I was surprised by how happy he was to see me. I was more surprised by how happy I was to see him, so small in the comical bed. It was molded plastic made to look like a race car, with fenders and headlights at the foot and large racing numbers and stripes on the skirting. The blanket said NASCAR. It had to have been a gift to the family from the Baptists.

As usual, Ali had not missed a word of the tale I read him. His eyes took them all in. I swore he understood words with his eyes. He was smiling as those eyes closed.

His mother had let me in the back door. She had done it reluctantly, but I had insisted her husband had given permission. She opened the door and turned her back so as to not make eye contact when I entered. She was afraid of me. She was afraid of Big Ali. She was afraid her husband did not know I was there. She was afraid her husband knew.

I had tried to reassure her. "Thank you, Ma'am. Your husband says I might speak to Ali. Would that be all right with you?"

Then she turned to look at me. "That my husband says you

may speak with the boy is enough. It is not my place to say." She caught herself looking at my eyes. She lowered hers quickly, embarrassed.

"I would like your permission, Ma'am." I felt it was important.

Once again her eyes met mine for an instant. She was confused by my request. This time she looked back up, straight at me, when she spoke. "You may see my son."

"Is it true that Ali needs a new heart?" I spoke slowly and softly. I broke the eye contact and looked at the floor in respect. "Will he be all right?"

She sighed. "I do not know. His heart is very weak."

For the first time I saw her, really saw her, there in that kitchen. She was wearing a long black cotton skirt and a white cotton blouse. Here in her own home, she was not wearing her usual scarf. Her hair was a lustrous black. She wore it up in a loose gather, and it brushed her neck. Her forehead was proud, and her cheekbones, seen for the first time without shadow, were high. I looked away, thinking I would offend her.

"What do the doctors say?"

She sighed again, deeper this time. "What doctors? There are no doctors anymore for him. My husband says pray! The preacher says pray!" Her eyes were intense, shooting anger at me. And I could see as she turned to face me straight on, she had been crying, as any true mother would cry. I could see it all now, without the veil.

I couldn't help myself. "He betrayed his brother."

She gasped and turned her back to me again. "Go see the boy."

"He told me who he is. He's drunk, and he told me."

She did not answer me. Her shoulders slumped. Her hand fluttered at her side waving me to leave.

"He told me what he is." I don't know why I persisted.

She turned to me. She stood up straight and measured the words she spoke to me, so that I would understand her clearly. "He is my husband. He protected us. He is not a bad man. Ali loves the boy. The boy is as a son to us. Ali is my son now. The man you despise is my husband." Her eyes were even more fierce than her husband's had been in the garage. "He is a good man. We were all frightened and in danger. Now we are here. God will save little Ali as he saved this family from danger."

"And Doctor Finch?"

"A holy man. Now, go and talk to my son. You are his friend? Be with him." She turned away.

And so I had gone to my Ali and read him the "Tale of the Three." And his eyes had followed every word. And then his eyes had closed, and I became very afraid. I opened the book again in my shaking hands. Ali's eyes were closed, and they did not flutter. The blankets on his chest did not move enough to see. The little brown one was floating in his plastic bed. I would read him another story. There had to be enough time for another tale. There had to be.

We hadn't reached the end of the book yet.

XXXVIII
The Tale of Sin

Our boat sailed upon the sea until it became an ocean, and there was no land. The horizon became a circle around us. We were in the center of all things. The day was the blue of Farewell's water jar.

And the wind stopped. There was no need for hand on tiller or the cotton of our sail. The wind stopped, and we beheld the world as a ball that our hands or our souls could not encompass. All was beyond us, and all was made clear.

My Master and I drifted in the boat and spoke of many things. But one thing remains in my heart, and I press the marks into the soft clay of the tablet to tell you.

There were flying fish that day, and they jumped into our boat so that they could give us their lives as food and their blood as water. We ate and we drank and were grateful to the sea and its wisdom.

My Master belched as one does to praise a cook at a great feast, and his kind face was upon mine in gaze and in his words.

For thus, he spoke to me, "I have told you stories, brown one. Now, as a proper friend, trade me one of yours. Tell me of your greatest sin."

And so I told my Master of my sin. And this is my tale:

Now in those days of childhood, I played in the hills of my youth. I threw stones at frogs and nested in trees with the green birds who hide in the fruit and the pods. I swam in quiet pools and slept under that younger sun so that my skin was brown as a tangle nut shell.

And on Summer's Day, my sister and I jumped over the stream that separated farm and wood. She carried flowers and fruit. I carried bow and arrow. And we ventured beneath the branches and beneath the shadows that lie there. And many sounds unknown came to my ears.

I heard rustling leaf and cracking stick. I heard grinding stone and skittering pebble. I heard muscled breath and growl. And I trembled.

My sister touched my hand and said to me, "Do not tremble. You hear only the sound of the forest, nothing more."

But many new smells came to my nose.

I smelled rotting wood and sprouting seed. I smelled insect hive and turpentine sap. I smelled half chewed hide and meat eater's dung. And my eyes darted from shadow to shadow.

My sister touched my hand and said to me. "Do not look for what is not there. You smell only the forest's life, nothing more."

But my eyes saw strange events all around me.

I saw darkness standing, and burrows rise to their feet. I saw snakes flying on wind and vine. I saw tooth become shadow and fang become eye. And I notched an arrow on the string.

My sister touched my hand and said to me, "Do not arm yourself. You see only darkness masquerading as menace, nothing more."

But I trembled, and my eyes moved from vision to vision without rest, and I pulled the arrow back on its bowstring and stood ready for battle.

My sister laughed and said to me, "I will show you the truth of this forest."

And she went into the bushes that surrounded us, and she went into the darkness, and she disappeared from my eye in speckled shadow of dark green.

I beheld the shaking of the branches and the roar of the lion, and I smelled his breath and heard his claws on the ground and in her flesh.

Then, did I scream and launch my arrow, and true it flew into those darkened places and struck home.

My sister cried to me, "You have shot me, brother. You have shot me with your arrow."

Into the bushes I went, and I found her there. My arrow was deep in her shoulder, and she bled from the wound. Her blood flowed onto the flowers in her hand and the fruit in her gathered dress. At her feet was a hare and the hare looked at me in sadness.

Then the hare spoke to me. "You have killed my children in sport, brown one. Killed them and not even taken them to your table. You have done this in the light of open fields. Now, in the shadow of the wood, you have shot your own sister. I am sad for you."

With those words did the hare wound me, and the hare darted away.

And my sister said to me, "Now carry me home, brother. Carry me home, and see to my healing."

Leaving flower and fruit and bow and arrows behind us, I carried my sister home and gave her into my mother's arms for healing. In a month she was healed. But I carry the arrow of my sin still. For in killing, have I sinned.

Those were the words of my tale.

*My Master said to me, "Killing was not your sin, brown one.
Man may kill. Man may be killed. This time and life allow for all things.
Your sin was not in the killing."*

*So, I asked my Master, "What, then, was my sin? What is the
greatest sin?"*

And my Master spoke. "Fear."

*My Master and I floated in that boat, and he repeated to my ears
my greatest sin.*

"Fear is the greatest sin. Take care to remember this."

       And so I have, and so I have told this to you.

XXXIX
A Window

A flash of lightning lit up Ali's bedroom window.

His face tightened, and he grabbed at my hand. It scared me. His brown eyes bore into me. "Master," he said. I could barely hear him. His voice was weak, and his hand was cold. Though Ali's skin was brown, he was purplish on his lips. "Master," he said again.

I caught at a sob before it could escape. "Yes, Ali. You are my Master."

Ali smiled weakly and shook his head ever so slightly. "No."

"How is my nephew!"

I jumped as the door flew open, and Big Ali's drunken voice shook the room. I could smell the beer and worse from his blood spattered work clothes. A small tear drifted out of Ali's eye. It was curious, though. The boy did not look upset, not really.

Big Ali sat down heavily on the end of the bed. "My nephew, my son, how are you? Is your nice man friend taking care of you?" The drunken man turned his rheumy eyes on me. "Are you praying for him?"

Ali's voice was soft but clear. "Uncle, hello. Hello, dear uncle."

The big man's face softened. He rested his calloused hand on the outline of the boy's leg under the blankets. "Hello, Ali. How are you, my son? Yes, you are my son now. How are you?" Now there might have even been a tear in Big Ali's eye, too.

"I have been reading to him."

Big Ali looked from the boy to the book I was holding. "You read from the Master's book, eh?"

"Yes. Ali and I found it this morning. It has been our guide through the day."

"Master," piped in Ali.

I handed the book to Big Ali. He examined the worn volume carefully, like it was a land mine that might go off if he turned the wrong page the wrong way in his hands. "Doctor Finch showed me this book a long time ago." He handed the tales back to me and wiped his fingers absentmindedly on his work smock. "There is wisdom in this book. But there is no God in the stories. You will find no answers for my boy in those pages."

"Maybe you're right. Maybe there are no answers." I opened the book.

Ali saw the next page and insisted, "Read to me. Read to me."

The big man stood up. "Do you do what the boy says to do?"

I smiled up at him. "Well, I guess I do. According to the book, he is my Master."

"Hah! You see how crazy this is? How can my son be your Master? He barely speaks English. And he is..." He caught himself.

I looked at little Ali. It was all right. "He is dying? Is that what you were going to say?"

Big Ali was crying now. "No, please, not in front of the boy. Please. Not in front of my son." He dropped to his knees. "Please." He took Ali's hand in his, and he sobbed. "Please, don't die, my son. You must forgive me." He grabbed my hand. "Please, don't let my son die without forgiving me. You are his Master. Do not let him die now." The bed shook with his weeping.

The man was wrong about who was the Master. "I don't know what I can do for him."

The big man buried his face on the bed next to the little boy. His voice was muffled by the mattress. "Please help him. I have done so many bad things in my life. God is punishing me for my sins now, by hurting this boy. I will be the cause of this death, and I cannot bear another death on my soul. Do you understand me?"

I laid my hand on his back. "I do. I do understand you. Death is impossible to bear. But this death is not on you." I actually did understand something in that moment. I actually felt a small seed of forgiveness stir inside me. Why had it come so late?

Ali put his small hand on top of his uncle's shaking head. "Do not cry, dear uncle." Ali stroked his uncle's hair. "You are my Papa now. Listen to the story, Papa. Listen."

When he said the word, "Papa." There was forgiveness in it. The big man sobbed at the sound of it. "Papa."

I finally could recognize true forgiveness. The boy's eyes looked at me then. I knew what he wanted.

I opened the little purple book, as my Master had bid me to do.

XL
The Tale of
How It Came to End

On that day, we came to the end of the ocean. And the day was an arch of all colors.

Our boat had floated without wind or wave for days beyond days. And we came to the end of the great waters. The waters flowed over the edge of the earth. There was no roar and no thunder. There was no crashing chaos or foam nor spray. There were no more rocks to stir the tides and no shore to stop the way of the waves. The waters flowed in a silent curtain over that place and into nothingness, as the sigh of long grass on a still day in the high meadows.

We were in the place of endless quiet, and my Master's face was calm, and his body without strain. I then beheld his true age and saw the ending in his eyes.

And I asked my Master, "Is this the end of our journey, Master?"

He smiled with his hen's egg teeth and told me, "You have not looked for this, have you?"

I replied, "No, Master, I have not looked for this day. But I have known it was coming. For I have learned many things."

My Master asked me then, "And what have you learned, brown one?"

I remembered our travels then. I considered what I had learned. When I saw the lesson before me I spoke it, "I have learned to walk."

And my Master laughed until I joined him in laughter, and the ending of the sea was filled with our laughter.

And then my Master spoke again, "You have learned well. But I have learned more and deeper."

I asked my Master, "What have you learned, Master?"

And my Master stood on his feet and stepped onto the flood. And the flood held him up.

"I have learned to walk also, young one."

For he walked on the water, and my eyes rejoiced at the sight.

"You have learned to walk on water, Master."

And he spoke to me with a great smile.

"I once knew a wise man. One day I met him at a mighty river, and he bid me to watch him, and so I watched as he walked across that river and then back to me as if he were walking across a flat field. And he bid me watch again, and so he walked across that mighty river and back again. He told me he had spent forty years learning this miracle. He walked with me a short distance and watched me give a penny to the ferryman and cross the river myself. I gave the ferryman another penny and returned to the wise man's side. I told him then that while he had spent forty years, I had spent two pennies."

Our laughter rose again, and the moment was sweet.

And then my Master spoke to me these words: "I have learned about lost sons from a son whom I found. I have learned of a sweet wind blowing past bitter tragedy in the distant past and overwhelming the sadness. I have learned of children by a well. I have learned of true treasure and true pearls. I have learned what follows me beyond this gentle end. I have learned of magic and wonder and the taste of dung. I have seen a naked man richly clothed and an ugly man richly loved. I have held a forest in my hand. I have lived beside a prophet and given life to one who takes life. I have walked past the gods and learned the joy of Farewell. So now I say it to you, and listen well to my words."

And I said, "I am listening, and I hear your words, Master."

And the man stood on the very last inch of the waters above nothingness. And he said to me these words: "You are my Master, and so you have always been my Master."

I bid him wait and asked him, "But how is it so that I am your Master? Have I not called you Master? Have I not followed you? Have I not learned from you and done your bidding?"

And from the edge he spoke, "Did I not ask you so long ago beside a well, did I not ask you to lead me? Did you not lead me? Brown one, you are the Master, for everyman must be a Master. Everyman must learn to be a good Master, and then everyman can find a Master. I will sing you one more song."

And the man sang to me in the voice of a thousand birds.

A Master is not free
for the Master he must be.
Taking every lead,
counting every bead.

The secret is so strange,
but true without a change.
Be Mastered, you will see
the path to being free.

Be Master 'til you learn
that each will have their turn.
For leading is all dreams,
control not what it seems.

Being Master is a door,
so enter, find one million more.
One million Masters will you see.
One million Masters set you free.

And he smiled at me with white hen's egg teeth and my heart was full. He reached into his belt pouch and removed the pit of the fruit my sister had given him in that long ago time, and throwing it to me across the waters, he said, "Plant it where you find your Master. For each man must be a Master and having been so, may find the real wisdom. And the real wisdom is in finding a Master. Finding that, indeed, all men are your Master. By finding a million masters, you may learn from them all. Thus will you begin to grow. So plant this pit. Plant it where you find your Master."

Raising his right foot, he reached out with it into the nothing and gave me one more song.

A waterfall ends
where white foam shatters the sun.
So sharp it cuts light.

*And as he reached with his right foot, he followed with his left saying, "I live
in Freedom. Farewell!"*

And he was gone. And so it came to end.

*I was a Master, and now I seek a Master. I seek a million masters. I will
plant my pit near their wells, and my search has begun with these words.
Each Master must tell his tales. Each Master must point to the path with
his questions.*

And so I have been asked, and so I ask of you now.

XLI
A Little Death

How quiet can a death be?

Big Ali's crying had stopped, and he took in the story, kneeling beside his nephew's bed. His neck bent, shoulders rounded, face pressed into the mattress beside the boy. The thunderstorm had calmed outside. Only my voice and the words of the last tale moved the air in the small room.

My Ali, my Master, had his hand on his uncle's head. His hand was so small and so still. I looked at his tender quiet hand and realized that I had been his Master after all. That's what the tale had so clearly said. Ali had taught me how to be a Master, and now I was free to find my own Master. I was free to find a million masters. I was free.

Little Ali's chest did not move. The boy was very still. We had come to the end.

Big Ali's head came up, and the small hand of my little brown friend slipped off and landed softly on the blanket.

We just looked at him then. Two men full of secrets and pain, one kneeling, one sitting in a very small chair holding a very small purple book in his hands, just looking at the empty body on the bed. Little Ali was dead.

I have seen death before. I knew that Ali's uncle had seen death, too much of it. Death is not usually a gentle thing, nor is birth. But this parting had been so soft, so quiet, like the waters of a sea at the edge of nothing. Like the sigh of grass in a high meadow on a still day. Ali's farewell was wordless, and so was I.

My hand replaced Ali's on his uncle's head. I touched him as easily as I had ever touched a man. He turned and looked at me.

I knew what to say. My perpetual confusion seemed to be gone. "Come with me. Let's go tell your wife. Come with me. Lead me."

Big Ali's eyes were red. I'm sure mine were, too, but we didn't weep anymore. His voice was sober now. "I cannot be your Master."

"Lead me."

"I..." He struggled to his feet. "I..."

"Lead me." I looked at the big man. Big Ali's eyes found mine. There was a change in them. Maybe his eyes were reflecting a change in mine. I only know that the world seemed changed. The empty boy on the tiny bed seemed to be smiling. His face was full of waiting, and peace had arrived.

Big Ali took my hand and led me into the hallway. We took the short journey to the kitchen. It may have taken us a year. It may have taken us five seconds. The women were sitting at the little table there. Women gather when death is near.

They were eating peaches. Georgia's eyes looked up and pleaded with me. Marlene wiped juice from her fat chin and nodded her head when she saw us. She knew. Ali's adopted mother saw us and slowly retied her scarf in the manner of mourning.

Hope was the only one to get out of her chair. Her skinny legs moving, with unaccustomed deliberation, like a funeral march. Her cheeks were smeared with the wetness of the peach she had eaten. And she was so beautiful, my heart broke at last. I fell to my knees in front of her and cried, as I had never cried. Hope held my head in her delicate arms. I smelled the fruit on her, and I wept. I don't know how long I wept. I only knew that it had been too long since I had felt what I felt that moment, those arms around my neck.

Then Hope stepped back from me, just a half step, and holding my face in her hands said to me in the clearest of voices so that I would not miss her meaning, "Farewell."

The sound in my head echoed with a magic that went beyond the wisdom of the tales. Time stopped, rolled back, and started again.

She looked into me. She spoke in the sweetest of voices. "Farewell."

She stepped back, let go of my face and reached down to take my hand. The little girl with the dark brunette hair and olive skin turned my hand over and gently placed a dripping peach pit in my hand. She closed my fingers around it and said, "I live in freedom. Farewell."

The deja vu swept over me, and I fell back as her words hit.

Hope stepped by me. She disappeared down the hall. I heard her tiny steps, deliberate, and impossible in my ears. I heard the door to Ali's bedroom close behind her. She had gone to Ali. She had gone into the boy's room. As the door closed and clicked, the truth seemed clear to me. Time stopped, rolled back, and started again.

How quiet can a turning be? I felt my life turn again beneath me. When little Ali had died during the last tale, I had felt the soft turning of my fate. I had felt the peace of finding a Master. I thought that was the end of the turning, the end of the miracles. I was so wrong. I felt the turning under me, stronger this time.

I looked at Marlene. I wanted to be right, but I was afraid to be right. This world was not the place for the truth I felt that moment. What I felt belonged in a dream.

Marlene was looking at me. "What is it, Cole?"

I had to catch my breath, but I couldn't.

Big Ali was holding his wife. There was sadness and love between them.

Georgia looked down in shame. "I'm sorry I said what I said, Cole. I didn't want him to die. I didn't want..."

I found my voice. "Georgia, don't you see? All your predictions are wrong. You are not to blame. All of your predictions are wrong."

Marlene's face lit up in amazement. "Cole, do you mean that...?"

"Hope isn't your daughter is she, Marlene?" I knew, and I thought she knew, but I felt compelled to say the words.

"No, of course not." She almost laughed. "My daughter is twenty, and she's in Des Moines. You knew that. No, you didn't really know that. I didn't tell you all that, did I?"

"Marlene, when you knocked at my door..." I had to go slow.

I had to breathe. "When I opened the door and saw you and Hope, I just assumed she was your daughter."

"I never said that."

"No, you didn't. You just showed up at the door with Hope."

"When I walked up the street past your house, she was there. She was standing behind that ugly hedge of yours. She called to me." Marlene had to stop and catch her breath. She felt the turning, too. "Hope called to me and ran to me and grabbed my hand and led me to your door. She said, Hope said to me, 'Talk to him. Please, talk to my...'...oh."

"To my dad? Is that what she said, Marlene?" I knew.

That glorious, fat, beautiful face with the reddest red lips, smiled in wonder. "Talk to my dad. Oh, my God! Talk to my dad! That's what she said!"

"Sweet Jesus, Cole," said Georgia. "She's your daughter? But you told me that..."

"I know, Georgia. I know." I stood up very slowly. I was dizzy.

"But she can't be." Georgia looked so confused.

"But she is," said Marlene. "Whoooo!" Marlene whooped like she had seen heaven.

"Yes, she is." I was very sure, so I just said it. "Hope is my daughter." I might have cried, but I saw the faces in front of me change. There was a light bathing their faces. Marlene and Georgia and Big Ali holding his wife were illuminated in front of me.

I turned and saw him.

Little Ali stood there in the doorway from the hall. He was as alive as any boy I had ever seen. And his skin was the richest brown.

Ali stood there looking at me. When he spoke, I knew what he would say before he said it. "She loves you." He held a small rounded stone in his hands, Tadesse's stone. "She loves you. She's gone now." He ran into my arms saying it. "She loves you."

How quiet can a resurrection be? The world did not need my questions. Life gave answers unbidden. Sometimes angels come without calling.

I cried again. The little boy was holding the stone I had thrown away. I hugged Ali as I had once hugged a little girl I had called Fiona. With a peach pit in my hand, I hugged him.

In my other hand, I held a small, purple book.

XLII
The Writer's Tale

My Master, one of my many masters, walked ahead of me across a pasture on that day, and he limped as he walked ahead of me. And the day was blue with June.

And so my Master spoke to me, "Wait up a second, I've got to adjust this god damned foot of mine again. On a hot day like this, the plastic slips in my sweat, and I can't walk right."

My Master sat down on the soft grass and with a tug, removed his foot, boot and all.

And I asked my Master, "I've got a handkerchief. Will that help?"

My Master replied, "Sure, that'll do."

He dried the stump of his ankle with my white linen, and he wiped his sweaty brow, and under each of his sweating arms. Then did my Master blow his nose and hand the patch of fabric back to me.

And he said, "Thanks, Cole."

Then did he reattach his foot and stand in the warmth of the sun. He spit into his bib overalls and pulled out a can of brown snuff. He reverently placed a pinch between his cheek and gums, and we walked on. For our journey was of import on that day.

And my Master favored me with a question as we walked.

"She came back, huh?"

I replied in truth to my Master and told him my story of yesterday.

"Yeah, she came back. Ali and I were standing in the front yard getting ready to head down to Honey's for breakfast. Funniest thing, Ali doesn't eat chocolate doughnuts anymore."

My Master said, "A mystical change in him. Death'll change a boy."

I continued my tale, "Yep, now he only eats apple Danish. Anyway, we were standing there picking our noses when Ali pointed up the street and there it was, a big yellow truck. And at the wheel the prettiest truck driver you've ever seen. Sophia backed it straight in like a pro. And she ran into my arms saying... Cole, you idiot, kiss me."

So I said to her, "Welcome home, Sophia. Welcome home."

"Was the story you wrote me true?" she asked me.

"As true as true," I said.

"She wouldn't let go of me, Jake. Finally, Big Ali harumphed loud enough so she stopped and we could get on with the unloading. I don't know if she really believes the story or not, but I do know that ever since that night that Ali came back, I knew she was coming back, too. I knew she'd be back, because I knew at last that I would live and live well, whether she came back or not. And when I called her that next day, I said exactly the right thing."

And my Master asked, "What was exactly the right thing to say?"

I answered him, "How are you? I asked her how she was. I asked her about her feelings and her life and her tears and her shoes and her hair. I asked her about her. Everyday when I called I asked how she was doing. Then one day, she asked me how I was doing. The rest is history, Master."

And my Master said to me, "Cut the 'master' crap. Funny how it all worked out. Ali is healthy now. Even Big Ali ain't too big a pain in the ass anymore. That's probably because he's a Presbyterian now. Your wife came back. No earthquake. Everything Georgia predicted was wrong. And even she seems happy about that. Wish that fat lady friend of yours would stop preaching to me though... C'mon, it's just a little further up this hill."

Our journey became steep, but our feet did not falter. Well, three of our feet didn't falter. For my Master grew impatient and popped off his fake foot again and proceeded up that hill on his stump. And we reached the top of that hill. And the top of that hill was lush with tall blue stem prairie grass, and my Master and I fell on our bellies and slithered like snakes to the very crest of the hill.

And my Master said to me, "Sssh! Be quiet now. Anytime now you'll see. Just be patient. I hear you and Sophia are going to Costa Rica?"

So I answered. "Yeah, in the winter we'll go and we'll..."

My Master stopped my words. For the time of words had passed, and now was the time of seeing. Below us was a pond. A simple farm pond reflecting the infinite sky on its smooth chocolate surface.

My Master and I looked down on it then, and I noticed a small blue flower growing among the grass by my face. The flower was blue as lapis lazuli. There was gold in its center, and its stem was the green of a lizard after desert rain. And suddenly from the tall grass, emerged a dove, white as a flock of sheep on a meadowed hillside. The bird turned its head and looked into my eyes. I trembled as it jumped onto my finger where it alighted without weight.

My eyes did not blink as the dove took the flower in its yellow beak and stretched its wings. The dove took to the air and flew up into the sun until I could see it no more.

I began to speak, but my Master gestured me to quiet. "Shut up! Here she comes! Sssh!"

She stepped out of the bushes next to the pond, Mrs. Frida Jensen, widowed some five years ago when her husband's tractor rolled over on him. And she was pale and round and naked. With each step she took into the pond my Master sighed. We watched her for half an hour as she swam and washed her hair and finally dried herself in the sun. Then, she was gone.

My Master said to me, "Now she's worth sobering up for, don't you think?"

And I said to him, "She is beautiful, Jake. Beautiful."

I told my Master the truth for, indeed, she was beautiful.

There are mountains and valleys and sunsets and seas, but there is a truth to a man. There is nothing so beautiful as the woman he loves. And when that woman is naked, creation is in balance. It's magic.

My Master spoke yet again. "I told you. I told you. You can learn a lot from me, boy. You ever need any more advice about that wife of yours, you just ask."

I told him, "Yes, I can learn a lot from you, Jake. I can learn from you."

Then he said, "She was something, huh? You'll never forget this day, I'll tell you that. You'll never forget the day I took you to see the Widow Jensen skinny dippin'. You'll always remember this."

And so I have, and so I have told this to you.

XLIII
Pura Vida

I don't know many things.

I don't know why my baby died.

I don't know how Ali lived.

I don't know where the small, purple book came from.

But, I do know now that I am as much a miracle as any tale, any wandering sage, any star, or mote of dust in this world of ours.

And, I do know now that we are all masters… should we choose to remember – remember who we are.

From the pages of an ancient book, I found that memory.

A memory of who I was… who I always had been… who I always would be.

And I remembered, Sophia, my wife… my other self.

We found a new home… together…

Again.

The baby was crying.

I could hear her.

My wife was out. I don't remember where. I was sitting at my desk addressing envelopes to friends and family and the world at large, my awkward fingers trying to be precise, putting Forever stamps onto the corners of pink envelopes. I just had one last stack to finish. The baby was crying.

I put my glasses on the desk next to a small, rounded stone I found on a farm once upon a time. I pushed my chair back, stood up, and went up the stairs. There was a ring of water on the wood under my glass of iced tea. Later, Sophia would tell me for the fifth or sixth time to bring some coasters into my office.

Memory is a strange thing. In my nose, I can still smell the mock orange blossoms in the vase by my desk that day. My fingers still shake with the same tiny tremor that began with that scream. That day I had a sprig of fresh mint in my tea. Just the way I like it.

The baby was crying.

I opened the door to her nursery, and the little thing stopped. She saw me.

…and she smiled…

I swear she did.

Mr. and Mrs. Cole and Sophia Seatstone
gratefully announce
the birth of their daughter
Hope Fiona Seatstone
7 lbs. 9 oz.

A waterfall ends
where white foam shatters the sun.
So sharp it cuts light.

-The End -

A note regarding
"The Book of Stone"

The translation of these texts from the ancient Median dialects has presented a unique challenge; at times fragmentary, and at other times copiously annotated by later ancient scholars in second and third generation copies and commentaries. It is difficult to be sure of the provenance of the various versions. Certainly, the tablets discovered at Gobekli Tepe by Aasanda Devabodhi in 1906 and cataloged as miscellaneous cuneiform "flat pottery" are the oldest of the sources and may be dated to as early as 8800 years B.C.E.

The original discoveries include complete versions of only four tales: *The Apology*, *The Four Wives*, *Hope and Darkness*, and *The Tale of God's Foot*. Some tales, notably *How It Came to End* and *The Fish and the Oyster*, exist only in later incarnations of the tales without comparable text or fragments in the original.

It can be documented that portions of these tales were adapted by many other oral and written traditions, from Mycenaean to Minoan, Persian, Egyptian, Caldean, Habiru and of course Mesopotamian. The mystical viewpoint, and indeed complete passages, may be found in the *Torah*, the *Qu'ran*, many Buddhist Sutras, the *Bhagavad Gita*, the Zoroastrian and Baha'i texts, even the visions of St. John in his Apocalyptic writings, and the meditations of St. Augustine.

The tales exist outside of any known creed or sect and serve as a window back to the spiritual strivings of mankind in its infancy some ten thousand years ago. They are remarkably rational and free of myth, reflecting a naturalistic, yet mystic vision of man's place in the cosmos, the world, the village, and indeed his place within his very self.

Perhaps the most curious aspect of these tales is the disagreements that always arise when scholars compare notes on translation or reconstruction of these stories. It would seem as if everyone who reads the compiled volume finds a different set of lessons. Each person who delves into the wisdom of these pages finds their own story.

Some have suggested that the book possesses magical or even miraculous properties. Certain examiners have posited that the book transcends time. These assertions, though attractive, have no place in the ongoing study of this ancient scripture.

Read them as you will. Find what you will find.

- D.V.W.

Acknowledgments

I want to thank all of the people who have inspired me, helped me, criticized me, supported me, worked with me, and put up with me through many long years: Wilfred Fangman, who led me into a world of literature • My wife Debra and the family who never let me stay "detached" • Marian Blue and Wayne Ude, who helped me to believe • Joy Johnson who listened • Janet Roberts who made it real • Diana Greenwood, my long lost guiding light • Kent Bellows, who always inspired and understood • Dana Buckingham, who kept the checks coming • Roxanne Wach, whose design and keen eye brought it all to life • Sandy Aquila and her camera • John Rickards, the best friend a Yank could have in London • Ganesh, who handled the obstacles • Kali, who simultaneously bulldozed and caressed my ego • Hanuman, my constant reminder of why I'm here • and agents past and present, especially Alan Guthrie at Jenny Brown Associates, who has kept me on the list against all logic • I write in solitude, but I am a writer who owes his words to a world full of writers • Pax.